WILDFIRE ENCOUNTER

Because she couldn't bear to see her mother turned out of her home, Sara had been forced to marry Rafael Savalje, about whom she knew nothing except that he was the most overbearing man she had ever met. Rafael's excuse was that his little daughter needed a mother—but even for the child's sake, how could Sara face the situation?

Books you will enjoy
by HELEN BIANCHIN

THE SAVAGE TOUCH

Marc Leone was altogether too attractive for his own good. Much as he infuriated her, Lee had to admit that; certainly she could not deny how much she was attracted to him herself. But she had to keep the whole situation under control—because nothing was going to deflect her from her real goal in life: to marry a millionaire!

DEVIL IN COMMAND

The only way Stacey could get the formidable Paul Leandros to leave her young sister alone was to divert his attention to herself—which she succeeded in doing, with a vengeance! For Paul's price was that she marry him, and far too late, Stacey realised that the price was too high for her to pay and keep her emotions intact . . .

MASTER OF ULURU

On a working holiday in Australia, Jamie found herself encountering the forceful Logan more often than was good for her peace of mind. She could not deny his attraction—but did he want anything from her but a transient pleasure and amusement? After all, what did she know about him?

EDGE OF SPRING

After a brief and desperately disillusioning marriage, Karen had managed to keep all men at bay for five years. But she was having rather more trouble with Matt Lucas, who refused to take no for an answer. How could she convince him that she didn't want to have anything to do with him, ever?

WILDFIRE ENCOUNTER

BY

HELEN BIANCHIN

MILLS & BOON LIMITED
15–16 BROOK'S MEWS
LONDON W1A 1DR

First published 1982
Australian copyright 1982
Philippine copyright 1982
This edition 1982

© Helen Bianchin 1982

ISBN 0 263 73863 9

Set in Monophoto Baskerville 11 on 11½ pt
01 0782 47471

Made and printed in Great Britain by
Richard Clay (The Chaucer Press) Ltd,
Bungay, Suffolk

CHAPTER ONE

SARA cast a swift encompassing glance at the number of people mingling on the lawn, speculating that in all probability only ten were genuine bidders. The auction disposing the last of the late Blair Adams' assets was an event for the curiosity-seekers, providing an opportunity to wander at will about the home of a man whose tortured, guilt-stricken mind had led him to commit suicide only a matter of weeks before.

That fateful phone call, followed by the presence of Blair's accountant and the news he had to impart, were indelibly imprinted in her brain. Her mother, the beautiful, vulnerable Selina, had retreated into a state of shock that seemed to increase as each sordid detail was revealed, and it was left to Sara to assume the mantle of control, sparing her mother all but the essential facts.

A soundless sigh escaped Sara's lips. Within an hour the solid white-plastered structure and the spacious grounds surrounding it would be gone. Her home since birth, there were so many memories of happiness and laughter, the house itself so alive and receptive, so especially *theirs*, it seemed almost a crime that it should fall beneath the auctioneer's hammer and be passed to strangers.

Out of the nightmarish events of the past few weeks one man's name had emerged to head the not inconsiderable list of creditors. Rafael Savalje; his business interest were known to be innumerable, his wealth garnered from vast holdings in real estate along Queensland's Gold Coast. Residing as he did in luxurious surroundings on one of the inner islands not far from Surfer's Paradise, much of his personal life remained an enigma. He entertained on occasion, attended charity functions, and his name had been linked with several socialites over the past five years. Information gleaned from business sources labelled him a ruthless entrepreneur whose financial acumen couldn't be faulted.

'Sara, everyone is going inside.'

Engrossed in her reverie, she had lost track of time, and anxiety clouded her expressive features as her gaze settled on the neatly-groomed woman at her side.

'Mother, are you sure you want to go through with this?' For the umpteenth time she voiced the caution. 'It would be far less painful if we opted out of the whole affair and waited to hear the result through official channels.'

A slight furrow of doubt creased Selina Adams' forehead. 'Darling, you're right—but I simply can't sit twiddling my thumbs elsewhere. I have to *know*, Sara.' A pleading note entered her voice. 'Surely you understand?'

Oh God, what could she say? With a mixture of bravado and icy fatalism she summoned a bright smile, caught hold of her mother's elbow, managing through no mean feat to enfuse some enthusiasm as she bade, 'Let's go, then.'

Resolve and an ironclad spirit were necessary to watch as prospective bidders picked over the items of furniture numbered in room lots, and Sara was forced to freeze her features into expressionless unconcern as the bidding progressed.

She wanted to scream out that there had been some ghastly mistake, willing herself to believe it was part of a horrible nightmare from which she would awaken.

Two hours later she stood pale and tense as bidding for the house itself rose to the figure set down as a reserve. A few minor items of furniture had passed to various buyers, but for the most part there was only one serious bidder.

It was all over in a matter of minutes, and as the crowd began to disperse Sara roused herself sufficiently to view the room's occupants.

Nothing prepared her for the shock she experienced at seeing none other than Rafael Savalje deep in conversation with a man many years his senior.

He stood at the far side of the room on the edge of her peripheral vision, his hard rough-chiselled features stern and uncompromising. Almost as if he was aware of her scrutiny, his head lifted fractionally and dark eyes made a slow sweeping appraisal of the room, coming to a halt as they caught her gaze, and she experienced incredible rage at the analytical insolence evident.

His photographs didn't do him justice, Sara conceded reluctantly. No celluloid print could reproduce the physical aura the man projected, nor capture the forceful vitality evident. Eyes as dark as ebony held pitiless disregard, above a mouth whose lips hinted at a ruthless sensuality. Even sheathed in expensive tailoring, his powerful frame emanated an air of leashed savagery that boded ill for anyone foolish enough to challenge him.

'I suppose we should leave.'

Sara heard the words and turned slowly towards Selina. 'You go on ahead,' she bade quietly, resolve strengthening her purpose. 'There's something I have to take care of.'

Minutes later she marvelled that fate had been so kind, for she didn't need to employ any subterfuge at all.

'Mr Savalje.'

There was no glimmer of recognition evident, only a chilling deference to her femininity.

'Yes?'

Now that she had gained his attention Sara launched into her attack. 'You do know who I am?' she demanded starkly, and saw his lips twist in expressive mocking cynicism.

'Blair Adams' daughter,' he accorded imperturbably.

'What are you doing here?' she demanded bleakly, and her fine green eyes deepened with anger. 'Was the chance to gloat too great to resist?'

One eyebrow rose in sardonic indolence. 'I attended an auction,' he drawled. 'Is that considered a crime?'

'You didn't bid,' she accused pithily.

'An agent conducted the bidding on my behalf.' His tone was noncommittal and barely informative. It was evident he found her a nuisance, but little more bothersome than a fly he could brush into oblivion at will.

'Haven't you enough property without acquiring this one?' Temper lent her eyes a fiery sparkle and brought a flush to her cheeks. 'Why *this* house, Mr Savalje—if not to rub salt into the wound?'

His eyes narrowed fractionally, then became hooded. 'You have an accusation to make, Miss Adams?' he queried silkily, and Sara retorted emotionally,

'This house was all my mother had left. Her whole

life was spent here. Forcing her out is like severing a limb!'

His expression didn't alter. 'You have my sympathy.'

'Keep your sympathy!' she flung incautiously, becoming enraged at his apparent indifference. 'It's because of you that Blair is dead!'

Dark eyes hardened measurably as they surveyed her, and she experienced a shiver of apprehension. 'I was not instrumental in your father's death, Miss Adams.'

'Not physically,' Sara threw heatedly. A shudder of revulsion shook her slender form. 'My God, I can't begin to describe how much I detest you! I'm grateful Selina didn't recognise you,' she added with quiet vehemence. 'It would have been an unbearable humiliation.'

Rafael Savalje's features were an enigmatic mask. 'Is there any point to this discussion?'

'After all you've done, you dare ask that?'

'Casting feminine emotionalism aside, perhaps you'd care to elucidate?' he countered icily. 'I would caution against making any slanderous remarks you can't substantiate, or I may deem it necessary to sue.'

His words temporarily robbed her of speech. 'You bastard!' she delivered shakily.

A muscle tensed along his jaw, the only visible sign of anger. 'Have you finished, Miss Adams?'

Sara lifted her head slightly, her eyes wide and clear as she met his gaze. 'You don't intimidate me, Mr Savalje. In fact, I feel sorry for you—a rich, lonely man with no compassion and little integrity. Are you instructing your daughter with the same values?' Genuine pity entered her voice. 'Poor little girl—I imagine she's surrounded with nannies and housekeepers who present her for inspection at allotted times to fit into your busy schedule.'

'You appear to be inordinately well informed,' Rafael Savalje acknowledged, and she retorted with unaccustomed anger,

'If I could do anything to harm you, I would. Believe me,' she added at his faint humourless smile.

'I stand in fear and trembling.'

Her hand flew to his face in an involuntary movement that sounded loud in the stillness of the room. Terrible anger flared briefly in his dark eyes, then his lids drooped fractionally, successfully masking any expression.

'Does that make you feel better?'

The sardonic query succeeded in ruffling her composure, taking much of the fire from her victory. 'Much,' she declared succinctly, and turning away from him she walked stiffly from the room, leaving the house by the front door and not deigning to look back until she reached the car.

'Darling, you were gone so long, I thought you must have come across a problem,' Selina began anxiously as Sara slipped in behind the wheel.

She had—in human form! 'Nothing I couldn't handle,' she dismissed lightly, switching on the ignition. Putting the car into gear, she eased it forward into the steady stream of traffic. 'Shall we stop somewhere for coffee?' She didn't add, 'before going home'. The small apartment on the other side of the city was utilitarian and reasonably comfortable. Certainly it met their needs, but it didn't compare with the house they'd just left.

'What a lovely idea,' Selina agreed. 'We can discuss my news.'

Sara turned her head slightly. 'What news? Something you've been keeping from me?' she demanded in a light vein, her lips forming a faint smile.

'Hardly, darling. I've only just received the proposition. But I think it's a good one, and something I'd enjoy doing.'

'You've been offered a job?'

'Yes,' Selina agreed with a gleam of satisfaction. 'Andrea Lucas has an opening for a saleswoman in her boutique. It pays well, and I love meeting people—you know that. And I do have a flair with clothes,' she added modestly.

'You dress beautifully,' Sara complimented with utter sincerity. 'It sounds marvellous. When do you start?'

'Would you believe tomorrow?' Selina gave a deprecatory laugh. 'I begin at eight-thirty, so we'll be able to travel into the city together.'

A slight frown creased Sara's forehead. 'Not tomorrow, I'm afraid. I have to attend a seminar in Southport, and a parent–teachers' meeting in the evening.'

'Of course,' Selina exclaimed. 'How could I have forgotten?' She spared her daughter a conciliatory smile. 'Never mind, darling, I'll simply catch a bus.' Her lips twisted a trifle ruefully. 'It's something I'll have to get used to.'

Sara negotiated a set of traffic lights, then moved over to an inside lane that would ultimately lead them to a nearby parking building. 'You shall have the car tomorrow. John is taking his car, and I can get a lift with him.'

It wasn't something she relished doing, for John Peterson had been a persistent admirer for several months, and the slightest encouragement would have him imagining she was prepared to offer more than casual friendship.

At twenty-three, Sara had been teaching junior grades for three years, and it was something of an honour to have been selected to attend the seminar. One of the guest speakers was a visiting dignitary from America whose views on education were held in high esteem, and coupled with an expert in child psychology, the event showed every indication of being an interesting experience. Children, their welfare and education, were very dear to her heart, and her genuine enthusiasm had the effect of bringing out the best in her young charges.

The following day dawned bright and clear with the promise of high humidity and stultifying heat. February was a bad month with the Coast receiving its highest rainfall, and the unpredictability of the weather tended to fray the most even of tempers.

Sara rose early and took a refreshing shower, then searched her wardrobe for something cool yet casually elegant to wear. After a few minutes' deliberation she chose an emerald green dress, strapless, its blouson top gathered in at the waist with a pencil-slim skirt split to mid-thigh. With white high-heeled sandals it created the effect she desired, showing off her deep golden tan and enhancing her delicate curves. In deference to the heat she swept her blonde shoulder-length hair into a carefree chignon, then applied moisturiser, a light dusting of powder, some eye-shadow and mascara, electing to leave the application of lipstick until after she'd eaten.

A critical glance revealed a mirrored image that was visually pleasing, although she had no pretensions about her own beauty. Her most striking feature was her face, its fine bone structure arresting, the skin smooth and clear, with widely-spaced eyes that were almost green with hazel and gold flecks. Her naturally blonde hair was thick and wavy, sun-streaked with gold highlights that added to an attractive whole.

''morning, darling. Did you sleep well?' Selina inclined from her seat at the table as Sara emerged into the small kitchen to prepare her customary breakfast of toast and coffee.

'Like a top,' Sara assured her, moving over to bestow a customary kiss to her mother's brow. 'And you?'

'The same,' the older woman responded smilingly, and Sara stifled a faint grimace. They were liars, both of them, intent on presenting a state of normalcy, aware that evidence of the tiniest crack would break down the careful foundations that were proving so hard to rebuild.

'Any worthwhile news in the paper?' she questioned lightly as she poured her coffee, and Selina shook her head.

'Nothing catastrophic. Rising inflation, rumbles among the unions, a threatened airline strike.'

'The usual state of affairs,' Sara remarked with a faint smile. 'I'll try not to be too late in tonight, but it probably won't be much before eleven,' she warned as she bit into her toast.

Selina nodded absently. 'What time is John calling for you?'

'About eight. The seminar begins at nine.'

'I wonder who bought the house,' Selina reflected wistfully. 'Did you see who the successful bidder was, darling?'

Sara endeavoured to keep her voice even. 'Yes—a

stranger.' That was true enough, for until yesterday she hadn't set eyes on Rafael Savalje's agent.

'It will take a few days before we hear from the lawyer,' Selina began with noted abstraction. 'I shan't really be able to relax until we know whether there's enough money to settle everything. There'll be fees too, I suppose,' she pursued worriedly, and Sara leaned across the table and caught hold of her mother's hand.

'Hey, it can't be too bad,' she consoled. 'Whatever the outcome, they won't put us in jail.' A light laugh tried to inject some humour into the situation. 'We'll be accorded a time limit in which to pay off the amount outstanding.' She spread her hands wide. 'With both of us working, we can reduce any debt without too much effort.'

Selina looked doubtful. 'Do you really think so?'

'Of course,' Sara answered bravely. 'Do I look worried?'

'Darling, you're too like Blair for your own good,' her mother told her with a shaky smile. 'He must have been stricken with anxiety for months, yet it never showed. Promise you'll be honest with me, Sara,' she begged. 'I really don't think I could bear to live with false pretences again.'

'Promise,' Sara declared lightly, mentally crossing her fingers. Selina was born to be cossetted, sheltered from any of life's unpleasantries. A beautiful piece of Dresden, delicate and infinitely adored, she was no more equipped to cope with reality than a china figurine.

Sara finished the last of her toast and drained her coffee, then standing to her feet she spared a glance at her watch. 'I must dash. If John arrives, tell him I won't be more than a few minutes.'

A quick touch to her lips provided colour, then she located her briefcase and checked its contents, caught up her shoulderbag and returned to the kitchen, to find Selina and John engaged in polite conversation.

'Shall we go?' she suggested coolly, meeting his open admiration with a faint smile before turning towards her mother. 'Have a nice day,' she bade warmly. 'I'll be thinking of you.'

'Thank you, darling. You, too.'

'I see you've come well prepared.'

Sara slid into the passenger seat and placed her briefcase on to the back seat. 'It's easier to keep everything together,' she dismissed, reaching for the safety-belt and securing it.

'You're very enthusiastic, aren't you?' There was a wry cynicism in his voice that Sara chose to ignore.

'Shouldn't I be?' she countered lightly.

'I hope it lasts. It rarely does,' he added, slanting her a glance. 'One tends to take a more jaded view as time goes by.'

'Perhaps,' Sara acceded noncommittally, aware that John's involvement with teaching lacked dedication.

'Your mother seems to be coping fairly well.'

Sara kept her eyes on the car in front of them as he joined the steady stream of traffic easing on to the expressway that led towards the Coast.

'Selina is very good at putting on a brave face,' she agreed, not wishing to pursue the painful memory of her father's recent demise.

'It must be difficult for her, in the light of——'

'Very,' Sara intercepted swiftly, her tone freezing him into an embarrassed silence. It wasn't the first time she'd had to parry remarks of a similar vein. Suicide seemed to arouse avid curiosity, and she marvelled at how many so-called friends and acquaintances could appear so intelligent yet lack even a modicum of tact.

The drive to Southport took almost an hour, for traffic on the Pacific Highway was heavy, and maintaining consistent speed became an impossibility. Sara refrained from offering any conversation, and John seemed disinclined to incur further disfavour, choosing silence as the safest course.

The seminar proved to be a success, and the hours flew as Sara took copious notes, her questions concise and at times challenging, so that she felt mentally drained as she placed sheaves of paper into her briefcase at the end of the day.

'A cool drink, followed by a swim, then dinner?' John suggested as they emerged from the air-conditioned building out into the late afternoon heat.

'Sounds delightful,' Sara acquiesced with enthusiasm. 'Especially the swim.' Her smile became an infectious grin. 'You lead, and I'll simply follow.'

'I was hoping you'd say that. I have an uncle who owns a fabulous beachfront home not too far distant. Strictly upper class,' he enlightened, as if wanting to impress. 'I took the liberty of ringing him last night, and we have an invitation to dinner. Nothing formal,' he hastened to add quickly at her slight frown. 'A barbecue, actually. And there's a pool.'

'The parent–teachers' meeting begins at seven-thirty,' Sara reminded him doubtfully. 'Will we have time?'

'Of course,' he insisted. 'I've told them we can't stay long.'

It certainly was a splendid house, Sara had to

concede as John eased the car into the wide circular driveway and drew to a halt outside the main entrance.

A modern edifice of concrete and glass, its interior decor was a mixture of cool greens and blues, off-white carpet, textured walls, and an abundance of elegant furniture.

Introductions completed, Sara was handed a tall glass whose icy contents slid down her throat with palatable ease, doing much to restore her sense of wellbeing.

'I didn't bring a swimsuit,' she murmured apologetically when John's aunt mentioned the pool.

'My dear, I have a daughter about your height and size who possesses at least half a dozen,' that good lady dismissed with a nonchalant wave of her hand. 'One of them is bound to fit you.'

She cast the older woman a doubtful glance. 'I hope we're not intruding——'

'Nonsense, my dear. John is always welcome, and you're not the first young friend he's brought to meet us.' She gave Sara a reassuring smile. 'There are changing rooms adjacent the pool.'

Sara allowed herself to be led to the rear of the house and out on to a splendidly tiled patio. Large potted shrubs provided a splash of colour among several wrought-iron tables and chairs grouped together at regular intervals around a large inground pool. An elaborate portable barbecue was set up at one end, and presided over by John's uncle attired as a chef in a brightly-patterned apron and hat.

'Our guests aren't due to arrive for another fifteen minutes, so you have time for a swim,' John's aunt declared, indicating, 'There'a selection of swimsuits and towels in this cupboard. Just help yourself.'

A few minutes later Sara stood facing the mirror wearing an expression of wry resignation. Uncovering more than she considered desirable, the skimpy pieces of white satin appeared a token gesture against total nudity, and she hastily caught up a short towelling jacket and slipped it on.

'Wow!' John muttered softly as she emerged from the changing room, and his swift appraisal was far too probing for her liking. 'Let's cool off for a while, then we'll change and have something to eat.'

'When you suggested a swim, I didn't imagine we'd be imposing on your relatives,' Sara voiced quietly, and he laughed.

'Good grief, you can't mean that, surely? Entertaining is their lifeblood. Most of Uncle's business is conducted on a social level. Aunt is so accustomed to catering for unexpected guests that the arrival of *two* wouldn't even lessen her stride. Relax,' he commanded, sweeping her scantily attired figure with an almost hungry gaze. 'Enjoy yourself.'

Sara wished she could change her mind, although to do so at this eleventh hour would seem a bit childish. There was little she could do except get it over and done with as quickly as possible, and with a careless shrug she slipped off the towelling robe and effected a neat dive into the translucent green water.

A sleek dark head bobbed up beside her seconds later, and turning, she swam with graceful strokes to the end of the pool and back, then made for the side with the intention of getting out. At that moment she felt a hand grab hold of her left foot, tugging her down, and she came up to the surface spluttering and endeavouring to catch her breath.

Of all the times to play games! she thought

furiously, and the glance she shot John should have quelled him in an instant. Except that it didn't, although this time she was more prepared, coming to the surface with some control, and when he would have caught hold of her shoulders she pushed him away and swam rapidly to the side, pulling herself up over the pool's edge before he had a chance to retaliate.

'Spoilsport!' John teased as she stood to her feet, and she summoned a smile as she reached for her towel.

As soon as the excess moisture was absorbed from her skin Sara slipped her arms into the jacket, and tackled her hair, squeezing its length over one shoulder before swathing a towel over her head and rubbing it dry.

All at once a strange prickling sensation made her turn towards the house, and the next instant she experienced shock as she encountered a pair of dark eyes whose ebony depths held mockery and a degree of cynicism.

Dear God! What was *he* doing here?

Why shouldn't he be here? a tiny voice demanded.

Without acknowledging his presence Sara turned and walked to the changing room, showered, then donned her clothes.

It took ten minutes to blow-dry her hair, and after applying a minimum of make-up she drew a deep steadying breath before making her way outside.

'There you are, sweetheart,' John greeted with unnecessary fondness as she moved towards him, and when she failed to reciprocate his smile, he slanted, 'Still mad at me?'

'Yes,' she agreed shortly. 'I hate being dragged beneath the water.'

'Oh, come on, Sara,' he remonstrated, laughing. 'You take things too seriously.'

She effected a slight dismissing shrug, and accepted a glass containing a tropical punch. Its palatable smoothness did much to restore her composure, and she allowed John to lead her towards the elaborate buffet set up at one end of the patio.

Several guests had arrived, and plate in hand Sara slowly circled the table, choosing a small portion from each selection, to all intents and purposes engaged with the matter at hand. No one else could possibly be aware of her reaction to Rafael Savalje's presence, *feel*, as she could, the fine body hairs tingle down the length of her spine, nor sense an erratic pulse-beat as she concentrated on avoiding him.

'Mr Savalje.'

Sara heard John's deferential acknowledgement with a feeling of despair, and only inbred politeness forced her to glance in his direction.

'I'd like you to meet one of my uncle's associates,' John introduced. 'Sara Adams—Rafael Savalje.'

'Sara.' He gave it an unaccustomed intonation, so that it sounded strange, and for some unknown reason her pulse leapt at the expression evident in those dark eyes as she forced herself to meet them.

It wasn't something she cared to define, and her response was deliberately cool. 'Mr Savalje.'

'Rafael,' he corrected with seeming solemnity, adding softly, 'I insist.'

Sara felt her eyes widen fractionally, then forcing a smile she elected to ignore him by turning back towards John. 'We really must hurry if we're to make that meeting on time.' Without a further word she moved away from the table and crossed to the opposite side of the pool.

'Wow!' John murmured quietly as he joined her seconds later. 'Do you realise who you've just given the classic deepfreeze?'

Sara feigned indifference. 'Mr Savalje?'

'You must be the first woman who hasn't fallen on her knees before him,' he accorded wryly.

'How—disgusting!'

John effected a rueful grimace. 'There's something about him that has women willing to do anything for so much as a smile—let alone anything else.'

'His cheque-book, perhaps?' she suggested with biting sarcasm, and incurred a laughing rejoinder.

'He has enough of a *macho* image to get any woman he wants—even without his cheque-book,' he remarked with envy, then went on to challenge, 'Doesn't he turn you on?'

'I find him totally obnoxious,' she said evenly, and glancing idly across the pool she found herself looking directly at the subject of their conversation.

Rafael Savalje's features were assembled into an expression of cool indifference, but even from this distance there was something about him that sent trickles of apprehension feathering down her spine. A man no one in their right mind would choose to have as an enemy, yet she doubted few could name him their friend.

Despite the warm evening air, she felt suddenly cold. 'I'm not very hungry,' she excused herself minutes later, discarding her plate, and glancing at her watch she reminded him, 'It's after seven, John. We should be leaving.'

He murmured an agreement, and Sara breathed

a sigh of relief as five minutes later they reached the driveway and the safety of the car.

'You didn't enjoy yourself much, did you?'

Was she that transparent? Forcing lightness into her voice she told him by way of explanation, 'I didn't expect to blunder in on a party.'

It wasn't long before they were on the main highway heading north, and Sara wound down her window to take full advantage of the flow of air.

'We'd better summon our wits together, I suppose. Our esteemed headmaster will want to be regaled with all the details.' John gave a prodigious sigh, and mocked a trifle grimly, '"Education is a serious subject, Peterson".'

'So it is,' Sara agreed sternly, disliking his cynicism. 'As teachers, we each have the power to fashion several young lives, and shouldn't take the responsibility lightly.'

'No, ma'am.' He gave her an elaborate salute. 'Have you anything else to add? Perhaps I should stop this trusty vehicle in order to take notes?'

'Wretch!' she scolded with amusement. 'Can't you be serious?'

'In exactly ten minutes I'll present the image of a dedicated educator of the young. Will that please you?'

A lighthearted chuckle escaped her lips as she nodded in silent acquiescence.

CHAPTER TWO

ALMOST a week later Sara followed Selina inside their small Mount Gravatt flat and secured the screen door, then she moved to the other side of the lounge.

'Phew, it's hot!' she exclaimed, flinging open several windows in rapid succession in an effort to dispel the stuffy atmosphere inside the small room. 'It has to rain soon, surely!' She walked into the kitchen and unlocked the back door, sweeping it wide and fastening the screen door. 'It's too hot to cook anything. Shall we settle for a salad? There's some tinned salmon we could have with it, and fresh fruit for dessert.' She extracted two glasses from a cupboard above the servery and filled them with chilled fruit juice from the refrigerator, then moved back into the lounge.

'Here you are—just what the doctor ordered,' she offered brightly, then she stopped mid-step at the expression of anguish on her mother's face. 'What is it?' she demanded quietly, crossing quickly to Selina's side.

Without a word her mother handed over the letter, and Sara's lips tightened into a taut line as she quickly scanned the neat typescript.

It had taken exactly eight days from the date of the auction for the legal professionals to determine and inform Blair Adams' widow of the sizeable deficit, requesting notification of the manner in which payment was proposed.

The amount mentioned was astronomical, and way beyond their meagre means. Even selling the car would do little to reduce the debt, and other than working out an instalment plan covering the next few years—Sara did rapid mental calculations, and paled at the consequences.

'Will they sue, do you suppose?'

She looked up slowly and spared her mother a glance over the sheet of paper. 'They can't extract blood from stone,' she managed with a faint smile that was meant to reassure. 'We've sold virtually everything we own; we're living in a comfortable but hardly luxurious flat, and we're both working. I'll contact Mr——' she quickly scanned the page for the required signature—'Shearer, in the morning, and arrange an appointment. I'm sure there's no need for concern.'

Fine words, Sara determined with scepticism as she emerged from the elegant offices of Sutcliffe Tripp and Finnegan the following afternoon. Mr Sutcliffe had been polite but firm—immovable, she amended a trifle grimly. Taxed with a direct query as to whether Rafael Savalje was his client, the lawyer had admitted as much, and it was all she could do to retain a semblance of calm as she rode the elevator down to the ground floor.

Moving out on to the pavement she crossed to a nearby telephone booth, where enquiries revealed that Mr Savalje could be contacted at his head office in Surfer's Paradise. A few more coins were pushed into the slot and a message relayed to Selina not to wait dinner, then Sara headed towards her car.

It took more than an hour to reach the popular tourist resort seventy-odd kilometres south of Brisbane, and a further ten minutes to locate the office block housing Savalje Realty. Parking her small car proved difficult, and it was almost five o'clock when she ascended by elevator to the second floor in the modern architect-designed block.

'Mr Savalje,' Sara indicated in a no-nonsense voice that caused the receptionist to blink before imparting that her employer was not available.

Sara issued a silent prayer for patience. 'Is he expected back this afternoon?'

'Possibly,' the receptionist replied, her expression doubtful, and Sara suppressed an unladylike curse.

'It's essential I contact him,' she said with abrupt importance. 'Perhaps you could let me have his home number?'

But young as the receptionist was, she had been thoroughly trained. 'Mr Savalje has a private listing. However, it's possible I may be able to reach him at the Southport office.'

'Please,' Sara insisted. 'It's important.'

A few minutes later it was determined that the exalted head of the real estate conglomerate had already left, and his whereabouts were unknown.

'Damn!' The oath slipped out, and Sara offered no apology.

'Mr Savalje has a radio-telephone in his car,' the receptionist offered hesitantly. 'I could try to reach him—although I've been instructed only to do so in an emergency,' she finished doubtfully, and Sara seized the opportunity with both hands.

'Would you mind?' She shamelessly utilised every ounce of charm at her command. 'I don't relish driving down from Brisbane again tomorrow.'

True, she experienced a feeling of guilt at the rather heartless method employed, but overriding it was the necessity to put Selina's mind at rest as soon as possible. Too much pressure and her mother might crack, and the consequences of that happening didn't bear thinking about.

Whatever her employer imparted succeeded in bringing a faint tinge of colour to the receptionist's cheeks, and her manner when she faced Sara was stiffly polite.

'Mr Savalje will be here in about twenty minutes.'

'Thank you,' Sara responded evenly, and crossing to a nearby seat she sat down and selected a magazine.

It was half an hour before Rafael Savalje appeared, and his presence set the butterflies fluttering wildly inside Sara's stomach.

After the initial flick of those hard dark eyes over her slim form, he turned towards the receptionist and gave a curt dismissing nod. 'You may leave, Karen. Switch on the answerphone, and lock the outer door.'

Grateful that she wasn't in for a verbal chastisement the girl quickly completed the task and left, and Sara viewed her departing figure with a sense of icy fatalism.

'Miss Adams.' The deep drawl was faintly sardonic, and she swung round to face him with the light of battle in her eyes.

'There's something we have to discuss,' she began without preamble, and saw one eyebrow rise in cynical amusement. Determined not to be made to feel at a disadvantage she fixed him with a speaking glance. 'Do you usually conduct business in your office foyer?'

A flicker of amusement was replaced by calculated speculation. 'I thought you might prefer maintaining a position of near-flight,' he drawled mockingly.

Oh, he was impossibly exasperating! The look she cast him would have withered a lesser man, but it had no effect whatever as he stood aside and indicated the passageway to his left.

'After you.'

Sara stepped quickly past him, and experienced a sense of misgiving as she heard the door snap shut behind her. It was ridiculous to feel trapped, but for one brief second she felt akin to the fly who inadvertently wandered into the spider's 'parlour'.

'Sit down.' It was a command, and it brought all her latent anger to the fore.

'I'd rather stand.'

On the defensive in such opulent surroundings Sara watched as he crossed to a large central desk, his movements lithe and indolent, then he turned to lean against its edge and his expression as he regarded her was impossible to discern.

Slowly, with deliberation that brought a tinge of colour to her cheeks, he allowed his eyes to conduct an analytical appraisal that began at the top of her head and travelled insolently down to the toes of her elegant high-heeled sandals, and back again, before voicing with damning cynicism,

'Well, Miss Adams? Precisely what is it you consider so pressingly urgent? So urgent, in fact,' he continued softly, 'that you would deliberately deceive my receptionist.'

Temper, she cautioned silently—at all costs she must remain calm! 'My mother received a letter yesterday indicating a discrepancy regarding my late father's estate. The result of your instructions, I believe,' she declared bitterly, silently demanding his verification. When none was forthcoming, she continued defiantly, 'You must be aware there isn't the remotest possibility we can come up with that sort of money.'

His gaze was disturbing, and she hated him afresh for placing her in the invidious position of having to beg his indulgence.

'I take it you are here on your mother's behalf?'

'Selina doesn't have the strength to do battle with a man such as you,' Sara told him witheringly. She watched as he eased his powerful body away from the desk, and despite the distance separating them his height and breadth proved formidable, causing a moment of sheer panic as she realised the vulnerability of her position.

'I wasn't aware we were at war,' Rafael Savalje drawled.

'The letter——'

'Stated a discrepancy between the loan negotiated by your late father and the amount realised by the sale of his assets,' he intervened smoothly.

'A debt you insist be repaid.'

'Naturally.'

Her eyes swept expressively over his rugged frame, and it was with difficulty that she held on to her temper. It wouldn't do to get on the wrong side of this inimical man. Despite the indolent amusement evident, he wore a mantle of ruthless implacability sufficient to quell an unwary adversary; his very stance reminiscent of a jungle panther—lithe and extremely dangerous.

'You have been told Selina disposed of all Blair's securities,' she informed him evenly, endeavouring to remain in control. 'Even to the extent of withdrawing personal savings, to which I added my own. Apart from a few necessary items of furniture and my car, there are no further assets.' She paused slightly, then became utterly infuriated when he refrained from making any comment. 'What do you expect from us?' she demanded incautiously, her fine green eyes sparking brilliant fire. 'We can't manufacture money out of thin air!'

His deliberation was incalculably intent, designed, Sara felt sure, to make her feel at a disadvantage, and it was all she could do not to resort to a childish expression of defiance.

'You have some suggestion to make regarding reparation?' he queried at last, and she took a deep steadying breath before responding.

'Both Selina and I draw wages,' she told him stoically. 'We could reduce the debt by regular monthly instalments.'

His expression didn't alter. 'What figure do you have in mind?'

Sara did a rapid mental calculation. 'Between four and five hundred dollars.'

'Your dedication is laudable, although unrealistic,' he drawled, his gaze unwavering. 'May I ask if your mother is equally willing to commit her finances so far into the future?'

'Selina would be the last person to balk at an obligation,' Sara flared, and saw one eyebrow lift with faint mockery.

'You have, of course, discussed it with her?'

'I don't need to,' she dismissed with a growing sense of irritation.

'What if I consider your offer unsatisfactory?'

'Damn you! What do you want?' she demanded angrily. 'Must I beg?' Her voice rose a fraction. 'Isn't it enough that you've reduced my mother to an emotional wreck?' Every ounce of fury projected itself from her body so that her entire being radiated with it.

Rafael Savalje extracted a slim gold case from an inside pocket of his jacket and withdrew a cigarette, lit it with a matching lighter, then returned both with unhurried ease. 'Your mother suffers indifferent health?'

'Why do you ask? Are you afraid it will take even longer to receive your money?' Her chin lifted in an unconscious gesture of defiance. 'I'll ensure you're repaid every last cent, with interest—even if it kills me!'

'You're being overly dramatic,' he drawled, subjecting her to an unwavering scrutiny. 'It's possible we can reach a compromise.'

'What do you have in mind?' Her temper was about to erupt, and her cheeks became pink with the effort of controlling it. 'Or perhaps I shouldn't be so naïve,' she said bitterly, anger flowing out of every pore.

'That's an evocative thought,' Rafael Savalje drawled with sardonic amusement, and without thought her hand flew to his face.

The next moment she cried out with pain as a stinging slap caught her left cheek.

'Bastard!' she choked as she lifted an unsteady hand to her face.

His lips twisted into a grim smile. 'As I was born within the legal bonds of matrimony, that particular descriptive is unmerited.'

'I find it particularly apt!'

'A dark angel, hm?'

'*Yes!*'

His scrutiny seemed to last for ever, and it was she who was the first to glance away, unable to hold that dark inimical gaze a second longer.

'What if I were to suggest that I might be prepared to let your mother occupy her former home, rent-free, for her lifetime?'

'In return for what—*me*?' she demanded with unaccustomed truculence.

'Yes,' he affirmed with silky detachment.

'You have to be mad!' Sara allowed her eyes to rake his powerful frame with ill-concealed contempt. 'Won't some other woman do?' A scornful laugh left her lips. 'I can't believe you lack for feminine——' she paused, then concluded delicately, 'attention.'

'No,' he allowed sardonically. 'However, the women of my acquaintance, while providing adequate sexual assuagement, appear sadly lacking in the one qualification I consider all-important.'

'I can't wait to hear what that might be,' Sara declared trenchantly, and saw his dark eyes harden measurably.

'The capacity to have a genuine regard for my daughter,' he revealed, and she demanded baldly, 'Why? Is she some sort of misfit?'

A slight humourless smile twisted his lips. 'On the contrary. Ana's only need is a reasonable quota of maternal affection.'

'Dear God, you want me to play *mother*?'

'Is the idea so abhorrent?' Rafael Savalje parried smoothly.

'That's the deal?' she queried in open disbelief.

'With one or two reservations—yes.'

'You'd better elaborate,' Sara demanded fiercely, unable to feel anything other than bitter enmity for the man standing opposite.

'You don't totally discount the idea?' he mocked, and one eyebrow slanted in cynical amusement.

'Cut out the word-play, Mr Savalje,' she snapped

scathingly, and her eyes filled with impotent rage. 'You require my services as a live-in nanny, is that right?'

'I distinctly specified "mother", did I not?'

'To be that, I would have to marry you.' Sara voiced her thoughts aloud without having any intention of doing so, and her face suddenly paled as she glimpsed the brief inclination of his head.

'You comprehend, I see.' His tone held cynical amusement.

'You can't be serious,' she whispered aghast, and caught the grim twist of his mouth.

'I am assured by various sources that you possess what is termed a natural empathy with children,' he told her hardily.

'You've had me investigated?' she demanded incredulously. 'How dare you!'

His eyes narrowed fractionally. 'Can you deny that you were equally curious about your late father's so-called aggressor?'

A telling colour flooded her cheeks, then left it as she became filled with quivering rage. 'At least you admit hounding him towards an untimely grave!'

A muscle tightened along his jaw. 'I provided financial backing on a business deal Blair Adams initiated,' he revealed bleakly. 'Without my sanction, your father made a quick sale and then reinvested on an unsound property, utilising my money and negotiating further finance at exorbitant interest rates. He was forced to sell at a considerable loss, yet he plunged into a further deal which rebounded with disastrous consequences.' His eyes held hers with unwavering scrutiny. 'He appealed to me for an extension of the original loan, which I refused. I regret to say he then made a last-ditch effort to recoup his losses, which only intensified his position.' He thrust one hand into his jacket pocket and extracted cigarettes and lighter, and his movements were unhurried as he exhaled the smoke with evident satisfaction before continuing. 'Contrary to your misconception, I was not responsible in precipitating his planned demise.'

'You don't pull any punches, do you?' Sara said bitterly.

'Your father was not only a gambler, but a fool,' Rafael Savalje observed hardily. 'He regarded your mother much as a collector regards a rare piece of priceless china. Her preservation in luxurious surroundings had to be maintained at any cost.'

'He loved her,' Sara cried in defence, unbearably hurt by his criticism. 'She was his life, the reason for his existence.'

'Yes,' he agreed with succinct sarcasm, and she lashed out in utter fury,

'You're nothing less than an unfeeling monster! You don't have the capacity to give affection—let alone *love*!'

'I love my daughter.'

'Perhaps,' Sara acceded with marked acerbity. 'Poor little scrap, I feel sorry for her already. If she's anything like her father, my task will be impossible!'

'You accept?' His eyes were dark and impassive, and she grimaced with distaste.

'I'm tempted to throw your offer back in your face,' she resolved with unnecessary force. 'Selina's resilience is extremely delicate. I don't relish putting her through any further anguish—in fact, I'll go to any lengths to avoid it.'

'Even marrying me,' he drawled, and her features darkened with expressive rage.

'*Yes*—damn you!'

His gaze was unfathomable, and it seemed an age before he spoke. 'Be sure of your decision, Sara,' he warned with dangerous silkiness. 'I won't allow you to change your mind.'

Her eyes were drawn to his, seeing clearly the grim implacability evident, a ruthlessness that sent shivers of apprehension feathering down her spine. 'This marriage,' she began unevenly. 'Am I expected to——'

'Share my bed?' he finished cynically, trapping her with his eyes so that she was unable to glance away. 'Why shouldn't I exercise a husband's rights?'

The thought of him as a lover sent her into an uneviable state of confusion. 'I don't find you in the least attractive.' The words held invective, and she allowed her gaze to sweep his lengthy frame with utter antipathy. 'What if I refuse?'

His expression became musingly speculative as he effected an indolent shrug. 'The choice is yours.'

'You'll allow me to have my own room?' Her voice rose a fraction with incredulity.

'No,' he refused silkily. 'You'll share my room and occupy my bed. It's a very large bed,' he revealed sardonically. 'I doubt you'll be aware of my presence.'

Her stomach lurched, then tightened into a painful ball. 'I wouldn't trust you as far as I could throw you,' she said shakily. Her heart began an erratic tattoo at the thought of sharing several hours each night in close proximity to a man of his undoubted virility. It was madness!

'I've never been an advocate of rape.'

'Merely employed subtle persuasion,' she retorted with biting sarcasm, and glimpsed his amusement.

'There is a difference.'

'Either way, I lose,' Sara said bitterly, hating him afresh.

'You require my sympathy?'

Her hand flew towards his face in a swift arc that never reached its mark, and she cried out in pain as strong fingers caught and held her arm in a merciless grip.

His head lowered with deadly intent, and the soundless scream that had become trapped in her throat suddenly erupted.

'Let me go!' Never in her life had she glimpsed such inimical rage, and fear lent strength as she struggled to be free of him.

'Barbarian!' Sara vented, her voice raw with anger, then his mouth closed over hers and she swayed beneath the hardness of his lips as they heartlessly crushed hers in a punishing attempt to force them apart.

Moving her head in violent opposition did no good at all, and she uttered a protesting moan as he caught her close against his hard frame.

Every attempt to escape proved fruitless, and she became breathless with the force of his kiss and her own exertion. Yet to stand quiescent in his arms was intolerable, and she rained her fists against his broad back, his ribs, anywhere she could reach, in an effort to be free of him.

With agile ease he captured first one wrist, then the other, and held them together behind her back. A hand slid to her nape and his fingers threaded themselves through her hair with little regard for her delicate scalp.

Defeated, Sara gave a gasp of impotent rage, and that unbidden relaxing of her jaw allowed him entry to violate the soft inner tissue of her mouth in a kiss that was relentlessly cruel.

Futility at her own weakness, the lack of sheer physical strength to outmatch him, exploded inside her, and when he finally released her she would have fallen had he not offered a steadying hand. For a few timeless seconds she was completely disorientated, then the numbness subsided and fury lent her eyes a fiery sparkle, twin flags of colour highlighting her cheekbones in an otherwise pale face.

'Don't look so—devastated,' Rafael Savalje drawled. 'I only kissed you.'

Wrath brought a husky note to her voice. 'It was a deliberately cruel assault, and you know it!'

'Would you rather I had slapped your face?'

'You provoked me,' Sara defended emotively, and his features hardened measurably.

'And I, of course, cannot claim provocation?'

'This—proposition of yours is a one-way ticket to disaster. I hate everything about you—everything you stand for,' she flung incautiously. 'What sort of foundation is that for marriage?' She lifted her eyes to his, but was unable to glean anything from his expression. 'How can you possibly expect your daughter to believe in something so false?'

'By ensuring that it doesn't appear so,' he declared with silky detachment, and she gave a disbelieving laugh.

'How do you propose to do that? By offering a kiss to my cheek, or placing an arm around my shoulder in her presence?' She shook her head slowly, and her voice lost its former anger. 'Children are far more sensitive to people's emotions than we give them credit for,' she expounded soberly. 'It's not merely visual actions or words. An entire composite of body language is necessary.'

'It shouldn't be too difficult,' he insisted impassively. 'Apart from weekends, it will involve twenty minutes over breakfast each morning, an hour or two in the evening. I shall help you.'

'Like you did just now?' she demanded with scorn. 'If that's an example of your so-called affection, then I'll pass!'

'I'm told I am quite—satisfactory, when I choose,' he drawled, and catching hold of her shoulders he propelled her slowly forward.

'Leave me alone!' Sara protested, endeavouring to wrench away from his grasp, but he resisted her futile attempt to escape with an ease that was galling.

'Regard it as an educational exercise,' he drawled mockingly.

'You—*savage*!' she choked an instant before his mouth fastened on hers, and steeled herself against another infliction of pain. Instead his lips were warm and deliberately evocative as they moved back and forth on hers, their touch insistently probing.

'Open your mouth,' Rafael said quietly, and she shook her head in mute defiance, determined not to fall into the same trap twice.

'Afraid you might enjoy it, Sara?' he taunted, and she gave a soundless gasp as his lips trailed down to caress the pulsating cord at the edge of her neck, then moved to seek the hollows at the base of her throat before travelling to a sensitive earlobe. His tongue tantalised a path over its shell-like orifice, then slowly his mouth moved to claim hers in a kiss that brought each nerve-end tinglingly alive.

Of their own volition her lips parted, and she was scarcely aware of her response as a treacherous warmth invaded her limbs, until it felt as if liquid fire coursed through her veins.

'We're not as incompatible as you would prefer to believe,' Rafael drawled with hateful amusement as he released her, and Sara retorted resentfully,

'I bow down to your—er——' she paused deliberately, then forced a light laugh—'superior talent.' She gave a slightly wicked smile. 'Becoming your wife may very well have its interesting moments.'

His eyes narrowed in thoughtful speculation. 'I don't doubt it,' he concurred mockingly, and a faint tinge of colour flew to her cheeks.

With hands that shook slightly she extricated herself from his arms and bent to collect her bag from where it had fallen on the carpet, then straightening she spared a glance at her watch. 'It's late,' she observed, noticing for the first time that the room had become bathed with the first flush of evening dusk.

'Have dinner with me.'

It was a command she chose to ignore. 'I can't,' she refused starkly. 'Selina is expecting me home.'

'Telephone her.' Steel encased in silk lent credence to the dangerous reputation the man had earned, and Sara experienced a frisson of fear at her vulnerability.

Anger at his highhandedness won, and she met his narrowed gaze squarely. 'You don't own me— at least, not yet,' she corrected with hostile bleakness.

'You show courage, Sara Adams,' he accorded ruminatively, and his lips twisted into a wry facsimile of a smile. 'I have you very much at my mercy, yet you choose to defy me.' He indicated the closed door with an indolent sweep of his arm. 'There's no one within earshot to effect a rescue.'

'I've agreed to your proposition,' she said unsteadily. 'What more do you want?'

Rafael took his time answering, and the silence in the room became enervating to the extent that Sara was aware of each separate heartbeat as she waited for him to speak.

'It is important for Ana to meet you, don't you agree?' His expresssion was an inscrutable mask. 'Having dinner at my home will provide that opportunity.'

'Must it be tonight?' The prospect was daunting, and one she would have preferred to face with more than some fifteen minutes' notice.

'The sooner the better, if I am to tell her of our impending marriage.'

'What if I don't meet with her approval?' Her concern wasn't feigned, and her forehead furrowed in doubt.

'Ana will wish only for my happiness,' Rafael Savalje assured her. 'I ask that you make it appear convincing.'

'Dear God!' Sara breathed piously, and incurred his twisted smile.

'There's more. Ana's grandmother is a member of my household, a respected old lady who has the welfare of her son and granddaughter very much at heart.'

'Who will examine a future daughter-in-law to the nth degree. You really are placing a cat among the pigeons, aren't you?' Sara demanded warily, then spared a rueful glance at her attire. 'I'm not exactly dressed to meet the family.'

'You'll do.'

'Thank you,' she acknowledged wryly. 'Just what I need to boost my confidence!'

'Dinner will be an informal affair,' Rafael revealed smoothly. 'We are not expecting guests.'

Sara stifled a sigh of resignation as she crossed to the desk, and sparing him a cursory glance she indicated the telephone. 'May I?'

'You can use the one in my car,' he drawled.

'Of course—how foolish of me,' she said dryly, and incurred a dark spearing glance.

'A word of warning,' Rafael intoned silkily. 'Behave, Sara. You wouldn't like the consequences should you dare to thwart me.'

'I shall be a model of docility,' Sara assured him with seeming sweetness as she preceded him into the passageway. 'Suitably enthralled with her very new fiancée, his splendid home, his doting mama, and his dutiful adoring daughter—both of whom obviously regard him as God, Santa Claus, plus a clutch of saints too numerous to mention!'

'You are a virago, aren't you?'

'I don't want to have dinner with you—in fact, I don't want to have anything to do with you at all!' She drew a deep breath and gave him a baleful glare. 'In my book, you're nothing less than despicable!'

'My heart aches,' he drawled mockingly, and Sara clenched her hands against a fresh tide of anger.

'You don't have a heart,' she cried vehemently, and his gaze became wholly cynical.

'I assure you I have all the normal requisites.'

'Oh—go to hell!'

CHAPTER THREE

RAFAEL SAVALJE'S car was a stunning white Porsche, and to Sara's jaundiced view the vehicle was a mechanical extension of the man himself.

Heading south, he handled its leashed power with disturbing ease, negotiating the early evening traffic with consummate skill.

'Call your mother.'

Sara cast him a cursory glance before accepting the outstretched receiver from his hand, and was careful to avoid any contact.

'Dial straight through,' he instructed brusquely, not taking his eyes from the road, and she suppressed a grimace as she punched the required buttons, her lips pursing as she waited for Selina to answer.

Aware that he could hear every word, she kept the ensuing conversation brief, and replaced the receiver with an almost silent click. 'Your turn.'

He slanted her a startlingly direct glance. 'It isn't necessary.'

Sara feigned surprise. 'An extra guest requires no advance notification? I'd hate to take anyone's share.'

The subtle sarcasm didn't pass unnoticed. 'Rest assured you will not.' His tone was dismissive, and she observed sweetly,

'Really? You must employ a very capable cook.'

'My household is efficiently run.'

'I'm sure it wouldn't dare be otherwise!'

'We're less than ten minutes away from my home,' Rafael informed her with dangerous softness. 'I'm sure you don't need me to remind you about your behaviour in the presence of my daughter. One word out of place, Sara,' he warned silkily, 'and you'll answer to me.'

'I'm petrified,' she answered glibly.

'Don't start something you've no hope of finishing,' he cautioned with grim implacability, taking his eyes from the road to shoot her a forbidding glance.

'Oh, for heaven's sake!' she snapped crossly. 'You sound like the classic heavy in a "B" grade movie! All that's missing is a gun pushed against my ribs!'

'Now you're being melodramatic.'

'Am I?' Sara demanded. 'I'm here under duress, which is almost the same thing!'

'You were given a choice,' he stated hardily, and she uttered a bitter laugh.

'The odds were all in your favour, Mr Savalje. Don't even try to insult my intelligence by insinuating otherwise!'

'Rafael,' he insisted. 'Ana will think it strange if you address me other than by my given name.'

'I'll probably choke every time I have to say it!'

'Practice will assuredly make it easier.'

'*Never*,' she vouchsafed vehemently, and could have slapped the acknowledging wry smile from his sardonic features.

The Porsche eased imperceptibly and turned in towards an impressive set of wrought-iron gates which swept open and then closed with smooth remote control precision the instant the car's wheels cleared the aperture.

Sara gave a faint grimace as she noted the solid

brick wall stretching wide to enclose spacious grounds that were landscaped to perfection, and her eyes widened with reluctant admiration as she caught sight of the elegant mansion resting in architectural splendour at the head of the gently curving driveway.

Mediterranean in design, its double-storied construction was of rough-faced cream stone, with glazed terracotta tiles covering its sloping roof. Numerous wide arches graced the forecourt and splendid balconies hedged with wrought-iron lent an air of dignity that was a silent endorsement of its owner's considerable wealth.

'You're taking an awful risk,' Sara murmured as she stepped out from the car, and her features became serious as the complexities of what she was undertaking assumed mammoth proportions. 'What if Ana hates me?'

His dark eyes were startlingly direct as he crossed round to stand beside her. 'My daughter is already aware of your existence.'

Sara's surprise was genuine. 'I've never met her,' she said positively. 'I would have remembered the name.'

'Ana was a guest at a children's party you attended several weeks ago.' His mouth twisted into a sardonic smile. 'You have been lauded with amazing frequency ever since.'

There were two possibilities, and her brow creased in concentration.

'The Albertsons',' he enlightened, and taking her elbow in a firm grasp he indicated a central impressively panelled door. 'Shall we?'

Sara pondered what would happen if she dared pull away from him, and almost instantly his fingers tightened until she emitted a gasp of pain. 'For heaven's sake!' she breathed angrily. 'I'm not going to run away!'

His grip lessened without expressed apology, and she wondered if he ever excused his actions, dismissing such an eventuality almost instantly. He was too pitilessly indomitable to provide a reason for anything he did.

Either their arrival had been witnessed, or the exterior of the house was equipped with an electronic scanning device, for the instant they reached the tiled entrance the door swung open to reveal a correctly-attired man of middle years whose deferential manner immediately identified him to be a servant.

Sara stifled the idiotic mirthful bubble that threatened to destroy her composure. Why shouldn't Rafael Savalje employ a butler? There was probably a cook as well as a housekeeper, she thought wryly. Ana's grandmother doubtlessly reigned supreme as a dowager matron, whose solitary aim was to ensure her son's household ran with the utmost precision. A black-clothed martinet of severe proportions rose unbidden to mind, and Sara gave a mental grimace. It was going to be difficult enough dealing with one opponent—heaven preserve her from two!

'Papa, you brought her!'

A tiny figure broke into a run across the tiled foyer and with a gentle laugh Rafael swung the child high into his arms and shared an affectionate embrace before setting her down to stand at his side.

Sara successfully hid her initial surprise at her first glimpse of Rafael Savalje's daughter. Aged between seven and eight, she was an exquisite child, with liquid brown eyes set in a delicately-boned face. Long sable brown hair flowed down past her shoulders, sleek and well-groomed, and her frock of sprigged cotton had obviously been chosen with care.

'Ana, I'd like you to meet Miss Adams.'

'I'm very pleased you could come,' said the little girl with a delightful mixture of well-mannered formality and engaging frankness.

Sara glimpsed the warning darkness behind Rafael's smiling gaze and cheerfully ignored it by switching her attention to the child at his side. 'Hello, Ana. I'm looking forward to have dinner with you.'

Dark eyes glowed, and an irrepressible smile lit her delicate features as she tilted her head towards her father. 'Does Grandmama know Miss Adams is dining with us?'

'I'm sure Tomás will have acquainted her with the fact that I have brought a guest,' Rafael told her solemnly before querying gently, 'How was school today?'

'Quite good, Papa,' the little girl responded dutifully, while darting a quick smile towards Sara. 'Sister Monique is pleased with my test results, and I have done my homework—even finished tomorrow's assignment,' she rushed on breathlessly, so that Rafael gave a low chuckle and trailed a gentle finger down the slope of her small nose.

'Well done, *pequeña*! So there can be no reason why you shouldn't be permitted an extra half hour beyond your normal bedtime this evening with which to help me entertain Miss Adams, hmn?'

'Thank you, Papa.' Excitement radiated from her small frame, and Sara could only wonder at the rapport father and daughter shared.

There was no hint of harshness in Rafael's ruggedly-chiselled features, and a warmth was apparent in the depth of his eyes, affection tugging the otherwise stern lines of his sensual mouth.

'How was your day, Papa?' There was touching earnestness in the query, and Sara was unable to prevent a feeling of affinity for Rafael Savalje's daughter.

'Varied, little one,' Rafael answered blandly. 'A few unexpected developments, but nothing untoward.'

Arranging a demonic marriage could certainly be termed unexpected—but *untoward?* Sara marvelled at his mask-like façade, at the same time chilled by the manner of man she was committed to marrying.

'Shall we join your grandmama in the *salón?* I suspect she will be wondering what can be keeping us.'

Sara felt a sinking feeling as Rafael indicated a double set of doors to his left, and it needed considerable courage to step across the parqueted floor. Very little registered, although she was fleetingly aware of elegantly carved furniture and ornately-framed paintings adorning the walls.

Silvia Savalje was the antithesis of the stern-faced matriarch Sara had envisaged. Fine-textured olive skin, finely-moulded bone structure, and exquisite grooming denoted a gentlewoman whose correct manner, although slightly daunting at first, proved surmountable, and after fifteen minutes of polite conversation together with the added help of some excellent sherry, Sara began to feel that two members of Rafael Savalje's family were at least human!

Dinner comprised several courses, with Tomás' wife, Clara, in unobtrusive attendance. Conversation rarely lagged, its flow conducted with such skilful adroitness that Sara could almost believe her presence had been motivated by express invitation. It made her wonder how many other women of Rafael's acquaintance had been accorded the privilege of dining exclusively with his family, then instantly discounted it, aware that his feminine friends would be discreetly entertained elsewhere.

Ana proved a delightful companion throughout the meal, her contributive comments and queries being advanced for her tender years. The natural empathy with her elders, and their treatment of her as an equal, was something Sara could only admire. There was no doubt that as a father, Rafael Savalje was without fault. In fact, Sara found herself trying to reconcile the man as she knew him to be with the smiling urbane host seated at the head of the table.

After the completion of dessert, Ana excused herself from their presence, albeit a shade reluctantly, and was escorted from the dining-room by the sympathetic-faced Clara.

'You will come again, won't you?' the little girl appealed with touching concern after bidding Sara goodnight.

'I'd like that very much,' Sara said gently, and received a beaming smile in return.

'I told you Miss Adams was nice, didn't I, Papa?'

Rafael leant forward and ruffled her dark shining hair. 'Indeed you did, *pequeña*,' he acknowledged tolerantly. 'I'll be up later, hm?'

'I probably shan't still be awake.'

'Pleasant dreams, *chica*.' His hand slid down to gently brush her cheek. 'Sara will visit with us very soon, I promise.'

'Lovely!' Intense satisfaction wreathed her expressive features, and placing her hand happily into that of the waiting Clara Ana gave everyone an enchanting smile. 'Goodnight.'

As a child, she was irresistible, and proved a favourable weight on the scale Sara mentally had tipped against the dynamic head of the Savalje household.

'Shall we adjourn to the *salón* for coffee?'

Sara met Rafael's studied gaze and glimpsed that faint tinge of mockery evident. 'Thank you,' she acknowledged politely, preceding him as he moved from the room. Now that Ana had departed, she felt it unnecessary to remain. 'I must leave soon,' she told him with quiet determination. 'I have books to mark for tomorrow's lesson.'

Silvia Savalje murmured a conciliatory response, and graciously declined to join them for coffee. 'It keeps me awake,' she excused with a faint twinkle. 'That's an advantage of advancing years—one can claim almost any indulgence against social precedence!' Her lips parted in a warm smile. 'It has been a pleasant evening, Miss Adams—one I look forward to repeating. Goodnight.'

Alone with her aggressor, Sara said briefly, 'I'd prefer to forgo coffee, if you don't mind.' She spared a glance at her watch. 'It's after nine, and I've more than an hour's drive ahead of me. If you would be good enough to call a taxi, I'll get on my way.'

'I will take you home,' Rafael indicated, his dark scrutiny intent and vaguely forbidding that she should consider any other alternative.

She shook her head in silent denial. 'Don't be ridiculous! There's——'

'No need?' One eyebrow rose in cynical enquiry, and his lips twisted into a wry smile. 'I beg to differ. Neither Ana nor my mother would forgive me if by chance some harm should befall you.'

'I'd appreciate a lift to Surfer's——'

'Direct to your door, Sara,' he insisted with dangerous softness. 'I won't hear of any arguments.'

'My car——' she began, only to have him interject smoothly,

'Will be delivered by the time you need it in the morning.'

'Eight o'clock?' she queried with open disbelief. 'How will you manage that?'

'Without any problem at all,' Rafael drawled sardonically.

'It must be nice to have so many underlings awaiting your slightest command,' Sara remarked dryly, and incurred his faint mocking smile.

'Shall we go?'

'An excellent suggestion. I can't wait to get out of your company.'

'The spitting kitten is back, I see,' she observed silkily.

'Likewise the diabolical barbarian,' she added with seeming sweetness.

'With no hint of a truce in sight, eh?'

'None whatsoever.'

They had reached the foyer, and when Rafael opened the heavy panelled door Sara moved quickly across the tiled forecourt and slipped into the passenger seat of the waiting car.

'Afraid you won't survive another hour in my company unscathed?' Rafael taunted as he slid in behind the wheel. The engine purred into life at a deft turn of his wrist, and once past the gates he sent it moving swiftly along the curving stretch of road.

There was no moon to be glimpsed in the night sky, and the only illumination was from regularly-spaced street lights providing a winking glow between wide-branched trees as they sped past.

Try as she might, Sara was unable to dismiss the cynically ruthless man at her side. A wry smile momentarily twisted her lips. Face it—Rafael Savalje wasn't a man *any* woman could successfully ignore! Living with him would be akin to sharing residence with a container of dynamite—highly volatile, and totally unpredictable!

'Ana shows herself willing to become your devoted slave.'

Sara turned slightly and could glean nothing from his dimly-reflected features in the darkness of the car's interior. 'She appears to be a delightful child,' she essayed with quiet sincerity.

'Unlike her father, hm?'

'It hasn't ceased to amaze me that she came from——'

'My loins?'

She gave an involuntary gasp at his bluntness.

'Have I shocked you, Sara Adams?'

'Did you want to?' she countered calmly, darned if she would allow him to think he had. Envisaging that virile body naked and engaged in lovemaking was enough to quicken her pulse and bring a telling blush to her cheeks.

His soft chuckle did little to restore her composure, and with an inaudible sigh of vexation she turned to gaze out the window.

Reaching the Gold Coast highway the vehicle gained speed, and Sara lapsed into reflective intro-spection as the enormity of what she was undertaking began to assume nightmarish proportions.

'Let me guess,' Rafael's voice drawled with sar-donic cynicism across the darkness of the car's in-terior. 'Your second thoughts with regard to our—

alliance have begun to accelerate beyond conceivable count.'

'Brilliant,' she said stiffly. 'You read minds.'

'Yours is particularly transparent.'

'I'd like to punch you!' she snapped with punctuating clarity. 'Preferably senseless.'

The engine was reduced from a husky purr to a well-tuned whisper in a matter of seconds, then cut out to nerve-racking silence.

'Why have you stopped?' Her voice rose with incredulous demand as she swung round to face him.

He shifted slightly in his seat and rested an arm on the steering wheel as he turned to regard her. 'I guess now is as good a time as any for you to display a little healthy reaction.'

'Would you consider divorce?' The stark query came out in a rush, and she held her breath at her own temerity.

'As we're not married, such a course is irrelevant.'

'You know what I mean!' Sara felt her voice shake with emotion, and she viewed its transgression with faint derision. Just when she needed an audible ally, her vocal chords elected to initiate strike action!

'Think of the advantages,' Rafael reminded her cynically.

'Like *what*? Being held in a security-guarded mansion with a monster of a man for a husband, and permitted little or no freedom?'

'You have scant knowledge as to what manner of man I am,' he drawled silkily.

'You're an autocratic plutocrat,' she told him bitterly. 'The acquisition of a wife is merely to obtain a decorative appendage, and solely to satisfy the social graces.'

'I can think of a more—satisfactory use,' he

drawled mockingly, and Sara burst into angry expostulatory speech.

'How typical of a man! Women, wine and work—it's simply a matter of shuffling the three to suit individual priority.'

'I'm intrigued to discover in what order you regard mine.'

Sara clenched her fingers into tight fists in an effort to control her rising temper. 'I'd reverse them,' she snapped without thought, and he gave a deep chuckle. 'Do you mind if we continue now? I don't have a hope in hell of getting to bed before midnight.'

'Poor Sara,' he husked softly. 'Are your young pupils worthy of your dedication?'

His amusement made her want to lash out at him, but his certain retribution acted as a temporary brake. Drawing a deep breath she threw him a baleful glare. 'I think you're detestable!'

'My heart aches.'

'I'll get out and *walk*!' The words were out of her mouth before she had time to think, and his silence nearly made her cry out as she sensed the leashed anger emanating from him.

'I won't tolerate any further displays of childish temper. You protest too much—at length, and to such an extent that it ceases to amuse me.'

Blind anger made her scarcely responsible for her actions, and her fists pummelled against his shoulder, his chest, and aimed for his arrogant jaw.

His husky string of muttered epithets were barely discernible, uttered in his native Spanish, and his actions to counter her attack bore suppressed violence as with appalling ease he caught each of her hands and held them.

'Will you never learn?'

'Go to hell!'

'By the sacred Virgin Mother, I may just take you with me!'

His mouth fastened overs hers with punishing, bruising force, taking possession and invading hitherto unexplored depths until it seemed as if he plundered and pillaged her very soul. In an agonising, timeless void she prayed for merciful oblivion, and gave a guttural moan of despair when her request went unheeded.

Almost in silent supplication her hands fluttered in an involuntary bid for freedom, then retreated as tortured spent neck muscles threatened to snap at her jaw.

Subtly, and beyond her conscious awareness, the pressure eased, slackening gradually to a provoking ravishment of a mouth too numbed to assimilate or appreciate the change.

She eventually gained her freedom when he withdrew, and he thrust her from him with a gesture of self-disgust. Eyes impossibly blurred with unshed tears failed to see the smouldering bleakness in the depth of his dark eyes as he subjected her to an intent gaze, evaluating the visible effect of his devastation.

Like a disembodied spectator Sara heard the muted roar as the Porsche leapt alive, and she was aware of its controlled speed as it took her even closer to home.

She didn't utter a word during the journey, and as the car whispered to a halt in the deserted suburban street she stirred and mechanically went through the motions of releasing her seat-belt.

Sliding from the seat, she stepped on to the kerb and pushed the door, hearing its dull clunk as it closed, then she turned and made her way up the path to the flat.

She didn't realise she wasn't alone until she paused at the door and delved into her bag for the key. Damn! It would prove elusive just when she wanted the wretched thing!

Without a word Rafael took the bag from her hand, and within seconds he slid the key into the lock, releasing the catch.

Silently Sara took the key from his outstretched palm and stepping past him into the lounge she turned and closed the door behind her, shutting him out of her sight.

CHAPTER FOUR

For the first time in weeks Sara had trouble concentrating during class, and more than once she had to ask a pupil to repeat a question.

'Are you all right, Miss Adams?'

Sara collected her thoughts as she glanced down at the little girl regarding her with earnest concern and forced a bright smile. 'I have a headache, Suzy, that's all.'

'My mummy gets those all the time. Perhaps you should take some aspirin.'

'I'll do that during afternoon recess,' Sara declared reassuringly, and directing her attention to the assembled class she said, 'Now, shall we do some reading?'

There was an audible chorus of groans at this announcement, and she picked up a book from her desk and flipped through the pages until she found the appropriate chapter. 'Page fifteen. Brent, will you begin, please.'

The remaining few hours until school finished seemed interminable, and never had she been more thankful when the electronic buzzer denoted the end of the day. As the children filed from the room she collected together some essays for marking and placed them into her briefcase, then stepped out into the corridor and made her way towards the main entrance.

The heat of the afternoon sun rose like a wave from the asphalt pavement, and Sara automatically reached for the sunglasses reposing in the thickness of her hair, slipping them down to rest on the bridge of her nose as she made her way towards the bus stop.

'Get in, Sara.'

How could she have possibly missed seeing the white Porsche parked at the kerb, almost right in ront of her nose?

'I'm on my way home,' she said coolly, studiously avoiding looking any higher than his forceful chin. Her fingers tightened on the handle of her briefcase as she made to step past him. 'The bus is due any minute. I'll miss it if I don't hurry.'

'I'll drive you,' Rafael stated brusquely. 'There are some things we must discuss.'

'Such as?'

'The time and place of our forthcoming marriage.' One eyebrow slanted with cynical mockery. 'You hadn't forgotten, surely?'

'I wish I could!'

'Get in the car, Sara. It wouldn't do to let any of your young charges witness their beloved Miss Adams in a fit of temper.'

'I've had a difficult day,' she informed him with unaccustomed bluntness. 'I don't need any battles, verbal or otherwise.'

'Then do as I suggest and get in the car.'

Sara eyed him warily, unsure whether or not to comply. There was a chilling glint in his dark eyes and supreme arrogance emanated from his tall frame. Attired in immaculate beige trousers and an open-necked shirt he looked totally invincible. Short sleeves revealed an expanse of well-developed muscle and darkly-tanned skin, and he had hooked over one shoulder a jacket that had obviously been discarded in deference to the heat.

'Wouldn't a cool drink in pleasant surroundings persuade you?'

At his drawled query she gave a careless shrug and stepped towards the car. There didn't seem any point arguing with him—the memory of last night's punishment was much too vivid in her mind to want a repeat performance.

As they left the Brisbane suburbs and headed south Sara spared him a puzzled glance. 'Where are we going?'

'Trust me.'

A mixture of colours rose above the parched dry ground of midsummer; the cool pastels of painted timbers mingled with brick as houses lining the highway flashed past her gaze. Frequently there was a glimpse of carefully-tended lawn and borders of flowers, sprinkler-fed with life-giving water.

They passed Beenleigh and came into Southport, and Sara turned a cool querying glance towards her captor.

'I have to call in to my office,' Rafael told her briefly. 'Five minutes, I promise you.' The car slowed down and turned into an adjacent parking area.

'I'll wait here,' Sara declared evenly, and he slanted her a sudden hard glance.

'Dare I trust you?'

'Not to escape?' she countered bluntly.

'I doubt that you will,' he observed dryly, and she stifled the retort that rose to the surface.

Damn him! she cursed helplessly. Like a butterfly she was pinned to the wall with no hope of escape.

True to his word Rafael slid back in behind the wheel after five minutes' absence, and his dark eyes raked her features in swift appraisal as he tossed a small jeweller's box into her lap.

'Your ring,' he indicated smoothly. 'Put it on.'

'I don't want it!' Sara declared with unnecessary vehemence, regarding the plush velvet case with about as much enthusiasm as if it contained an insect of suspect species.

'Now or later, it's all the same,' he drawled with a careless shrug, then he put the car in motion and eased it into the late afternoon traffic.

'You're impossible!' she snapped emphatically, enraged at his arrogant highhandedness. 'I must be out of my mind to have been swayed by your proposition. God!' She raised her eyes heavenward with pious disregard. 'It's nothing less than a hellish misalliance!'

'Which you can't foresee succeeding?'

'Not in a million years!' she denied with faint hysteria. The events of the previous few days were beginning to have an effect, and she felt shaky and impossibly fragile.

The drive from Southport to Surfer's Paradise took only a matter of minutes, although Sara was scarcely aware of anything as mundane as time. Her thoughts were too full of the inimitable, *savage* man who had taken over her life with as much precision as if it represented little more than another business deal.

Rafael slowed the Porsche before a high-rise hexagonal apartment block and eased it down into the underground car park, bringing it to a smooth halt in an allotted space.

Turning towards her he took the jeweller's box from her lap, flipped it open and extracted a ring, then he reached for her left hand and slid it on to the appropriate finger.

A solitaire set in platinum, the deep-set many-faceted diamond scintillated fire and ice, and Sara viewed its magnificence with wry resignation. Inherent good manners forced an acknowledgment, and she voiced the words with polite formality. 'Thank you, it's perfectly splendid.'

'Let's go up, Sara,' Rafael suggested imperturbably. 'I could do with a relaxing drink—preferably something cold and very dry.'

Her eyes widened as realisation dawned, and the look she spared him was openly accusing. 'You've brought me to your apartment.'

'You sound almost afraid,' he drawled. 'Are you?'

'After last night, can you blame me?'

'A Spaniard,' he began silkily, 'even by descent, possesses an inherent cruelty when provoked. You would do well to remember it in future.'

'That's an apology?'

'An explanation.'

'Are you insinuating that if I bow down to your every wish, I'll lead a blissful life?' Incredulity was replaced by a tinge of bitterness as she met his steadfast gaze. 'We react against each other like adverse alchemy.'

'You have only one option if you want my assistance in waiving your late father's debts and restoring Selina to her former home,' Rafael declared pitilessly.

'You're detestable!' she tossed in a stormy whisper, and he answered in a harsh drawl.

'It is not so much *me* you hate, but the circumstances that brought us together.'

Her tortured gaze met his dark impenetrable profile, and with a choking sob she reached for the doorclasp and slid out from the passenger seat.

A key-operated elevator whisked them swiftly to the uppermost floor, and in the lush-carpeted foyer there was only one entrance to be seen.

A thick panelled door opened to reveal a suite that was the epitome of luxury, from the deep-piled off-white carpet to the collection of expensive modern furnishings. Prints gracing the walls showed a taste quite at variance with those in his palatial mansion, and Sara couldn't help giving a startled gasp of surprise.

'Does that denote pleasure, or polite rejection?'

'Who could reject it?' she countered simply. 'Do you spend much time there?'

His gaze was startlingly direct. 'The occasional night or two. Ana accepts that the pressures of business necessitate my absence.'

'Ah, business,' Sara acknowledged with delicate emphasis, and saw his lips slant in mocking cynicism.

'I don't pretend to lead the life of a monk,' he drawled significantly, and she managed a nonchalant shrug.

'Of course not.'

'What will you have to drink?' He crossed the lounge to the bar, and Sara gave an expressive sigh.

'Something long and cool with a bit of a kick.' She needed some assistance to get her through the next few hours, and alcohol would effectively ease her shattered nerves.

'Why not take a seat and relax?' Rafael suggested with unaccustomed tolerance.

Relax? He had to be joking! Disregarding several deep-seated couches, she selected one of the single upholstered chairs and sat down.

Rafael moved towards her with a leisurely pantherish stride and placed a glass in her hand. '*Salud.*' His gaze was faintly mocking, and she quickly raised the sparkling liquid to her lips.

It was extremely palatable and very refreshing. 'This is nice,' she said with genuine appreciation. 'What is it?'

'Fresh orange juice and vintage champagne,' he revealed lazily. 'Its seeming innocuousness tends to be misleading.'

'Are you saying I can have only one?'

'For now. When we come back you can drink your fill.'

Puzzlement creased her brow. 'Back from where?'

'A shopping expedition,' Rafael enlightened her blandly. 'It is my intention to see you have a wedding gown that lives up to Ana's expectations.'

Sara's eyes flew open. 'You've told her?'

'She has high hopes that such a happening will eventuate,' he declared urbanely.

'I see,' she said faintly, and took another generous swallow for courage. Heaven knew she needed it!

'Do you?' The fact that the query was double-edged didn't escape her.

'Yes.' Her monosyllabic reply held resignation, and his ensuing silence seemed to become magnified out of all proportion, so that she rushed headlong into conversation without much conscious thought. 'I've met your family, but I still know very little about you. Shouldn't I be more informed if I'm to be your wife?'

A slight smile tugged the edges of his mouth. 'What do you want to know?'

'Anything—everything you think I should be aware of,' Sara answered helplessly. The alcohol must be going to her head. She felt quite *light*.

'Ana's mother died in childbirth,' Rafael disclosed without any visible display of emotion. 'Beatriz was eight months pregnant when she became involved in a car accident. They were able only to save the child, and for a while is seemed even her life was held in the balance. Praise be, she survived.' His features assumed a mocking tinge. 'Does that satisfy your curiosity?'

'It wasn't my intention to pry,' she declared civilly, and his lips twisted into a musing smile.

'Perhaps not.'

Sara finished her drink and placed the glass down on to a nearby table.

'Shall we go?' he slanted, his dark eyes unfathomable as he regarded her.

In one fluid movement she stood to her feet, and together they left the apartment.

At an exclusive boutique—so exclusive only one fashionably attired mannequin graced the showcase window—Rafael's presence gained such enthusiastic response from the well-preserved, elegantly dressed vendeuse that Sara began to wonder at the volume of his patronage.

'Margarita, allow me to introduce my fiancée, Sara.'

Much to Sara's consternation he draped an arm round her shoulders and subjected her to an intimate warm smile. It was all she could do not to blink with surprise.

The older woman's smile was genuine as she extended a hand in formal greeting. 'Sara,' she acknowledged. 'It is a pleasure to meet you.' Her dark eyes sparkled with sudden humour. 'I have been waiting a long time for someone to capture this *amigo*'s heart. So you are the one he has chosen, eh?'

Her attention swung to Rafael. 'You are to be congratulated,' she said gently. 'The little Ana is gaining a beautiful *mama*.'

'*Gracias*.' His eyes held a devilish gleam as he sensed Sara's discomfort, and as if to compound it he teased, 'And Sara, Margarita—is she not acquiring something other than a daughter?'

The older woman's answering laugh was decidedly wicked as she glanced towards Sara. 'I hope you know how to handle him, my dear. He is quite a man.' Her meaning was unmistakable, and Sara felt a faint tide of telling colour warm her cheeks. 'For shame, *amigo*,' she chided gently. 'Between us, we have made her blush.'

Rafael's eyes narrowed in musing speculation. 'Indeed.' He lifted an idle finger and let it trail down Sara's cheek. 'Perhaps it is time to get down to business, hmn?'

'*Si*.' Margarita nodded her approval. 'Come into the private salon, for it is there I have had placed a selection of gowns.' Her eyes narrowed fractionally as she scanned Sara's figure. 'You were right, Rafael. Sara *is* a perfect size ten.'

During the following two hours a resident model showed a seemingly endless parade of clothes. At one point Sara leaned towards Rafael and whispered in a scandalised undertone,

'I do possess an adequate wardrobe. I thought we came for a wedding gown!'

'So we did,' he concurred with equanimity. 'Are you bored?'

'Of course not,' she denied hastily.

His gaze held hidden mockery. 'Then appear suitably appreciative. It isn't everyone who has the opportunity to witness a private showing of Margarita originals.'

The selection of a wedding gown was narrowed down to the choice between two, and in the end Rafael bowed to Margarita's superior judgment. Sara found herself hiding an amused smile—Rafael Savalje conceding defeat was something she thought never to see!

It was after seven o'clock when they left the boutique and headed back towards the penthouse suite atop the modern apartment block.

'I must call Selina,' Sara murmured, and a momentary frown creased her brow. 'She'll be worried.'

'Ring from upstairs,' Rafael instructed. 'I'll fix a drink while you tell her the news.' His rivet-like gaze was swift and vaguely satanical. 'I don't imagine she knows of our impending marriage.'

It was something she didn't relish imparting, and given the choice she would prefer to do it alone, rather than have Rafael witness her answers to the awkward questions Selina was bound to ask.

'I think I'll have that drink first,' Sara decided a few minutes later, and she crossed the carpeted lounge to admire the view beyond a wide expanse of plate glass.

The evening was drawing in as the sun dipped low in the sky, and the panoramic vista of deep blue ocean, cresting surf and sparkling sand, was sufficient to catch her breath. It was little wonder tourists flocked here from all over Australia's vast continent and neighbouring New Zealand to enjoy the year-round summer climate and bask beneath the sun. It was truly a tropical paradise with a thriving business centre geared to the tourist industry and the needs of its cosmopolitan residents. Many shopowners were

Greek, Italian, Yugoslav, to name but a few, and upon walking down any of the many streets it was possible to overhear a smattering of several differing languages.

'Your drink.'

Sara turned and took the glass from his hand, taking an appreciative sip before moving to take a seat in a nearby chair. 'Thank you.'

'My pleasure.'

Now that they were alone she felt awkward and slightly gauche. It showed in the nervous way she held the glass, the quick infrequent glances she cast in his direction.

'Ring Selina,' Rafael prompted quietly when she had finished her drink. 'There's a telephone beside the bar.'

The ensuing call was apologetically brief, and apart from telling her mother not to wait up, Sara was remarkably uninformative.

'I'll tell her tomorrow,' she began as she met Rafael's thoughtful gaze. She lifted a hand to her hair and pushed a stray lock back behind one ear. 'I haven't any details,' she offered helplessly, and his eyes narrowed fractionally.

'In that case, you'd better have them.' He stood indolently at ease, a short broad-rimmed crystal glass held in his hand, and for a long moment he gave its contents his undivided attention, then he looked up and his gaze was startlingly direct. 'The church is booked for Friday at five, followed by a buffet dinner at my home for family and a selected few close friends.'

'But today is Wednesday!' Sara expostulated incredulously, and he slanted dryly,

'Yes, I believe so.'

His lazy mockery was almost her undoing. 'It's impossible to arrange things that quickly!'

'You doubt me?'

How could she? Rafael was sufficiently influential to arrange *anything* to his advantage, and that knowledge was damning. 'I have to hand in my notice at school,' she began with a return of spirit. 'I can't just leave——' she clicked her fingers expressively, '——like that!'

'You can,' Rafael directed implacably. 'Your headmaster is an understanding man.'

Sara was momentarily at a loss for words, then she shook her head in disbelief and demanded huskily, 'You spoke to him? When?'

'Prior to meeting you this afternoon,' he told her, and she complained resentfully,

'You could have consulted me first.'

'Indeed?' His voice held irony as he surveyed her. 'Will you deny that nothing I do meets with your approval?'

True, she agreed silently. Aloud she ventured lightly, 'You could feed me.'

'An intimate dinner for two?'

Sara caught the faint mockery in his voice, and fielded it neatly. 'Is there a chef de cuisine closeted in the kitchen awaiting your command?'

'No—an excellent restaurant situated on the ground floor,' he drawled.

'How—convenient!'

'Very,' he concurred dryly, crossing to the telephone. 'I'll have them send up a selection from their menu.'

The food, when it arrived, was excellent. Delivered on a portable trolley, the covered serving dishes were transferred by the waiter on to the

table, then ascertaining that everything was in order
he turned and discreetly left. An aroma wafted up to
tantalise the tastebuds, and Sara needed no second
bidding to take the chair Rafael indicated.

'Were you born here?' She dipped her fork into
the delectable seafood cocktail and idly awaited his
reply.

'No.' His eyes held sardonic amusement. 'Does
that surprise you?'

'You have only a very slight accent,' she declared
thoughtfully. 'I just assumed——'

'My parents eloped at a tender age,' Rafael said
musingly. 'From Andalusia they fled their respective
families' ire to Italy and thence on to Greece.' His
eyes assumed a devilish gleam. 'I emerged into this
world on a ship crossing the Atlantic bound for South
America, and I was almost ten when we left
Argentina for Australia,' he revealed with a faint
reflective smile, and it was all Sara could do to contain
her surprise.

'I had no idea your background was so—colourful.'

'I am a leopard of many spots, hm?'

'As mercilessly ruthless as one, too,' she evinced
feelingly, and saw his mouth harden fractionally.

'Of whom you are a little afraid, eh?'

Sara met his dark gaze unflinchingly.
'Intimidation happens to be an unenviable weapon
you wield.'

'Indeed?'

His silky tones caused shivers of apprehension to
scud down the length of her spine. He was a dangerous man whose unpredictability demanded healthy
respect, yet with every word she uttered she seemed
hellbent on a path to self-destruction. It was almost

as if some tiny gremlin was taking delight in causing mischief, for in the space of the past few days she had hurled inflammatory abuse and resorted to physical violence in the manner of a recalcitrant, belligerent brat.

'I can't pretend to like you,' Sara offered quietly, and Rafael subjected her to a long probing look.

'It would be to your advantage to try,' he drawled, his meaning unmistakable, and a slight blush heightened her delicately-moulded cheekbones.

'Try the tournedos,' he indicated with damning affability, lifting a covered dish, and she shook her head in silent negation. 'Oh, come, have one,' he insisted. 'There's an excellent béarnaise sauce that is Carl's *pièce de résistance*.' He leaned forward and proceeded to serve her.

'I'm not hungry.' She wasn't—not any more. The thought of swallowing even a particle of food threatened to be a choking experience.

'Then at least have some *bourguignon*. No?' His eyes raked her slightly flushed features and his lips curved into a wry smile. 'Being perverse will gain precisely nothing. Have some more champagne,' he bade as he topped up her half-filled glass. 'It will help restore your appetite.'

'Stop treating me like a child!'

His gaze became thoughtful, and far too analytical for Sara's peace of mind. 'Then stop behaving like one.'

Without a word she picked up her glass and drained its contents, then she took a small helping from each serving dish and proceeded to fork it systematically into her mouth without tasting so much as a morsel.

It wasn't until her plate was empty that she began

to feel the effects of the champagne, and she became more visibly relaxed with each passing minute.

'Dessert? Pears baked in white wine—I can recommend it.'

'Thank you, no.' Sara refused, giving a satisfied sigh as she leaned back in her chair.

'More champagne?'

Dared she? Perhaps another one, she decided. It certainly helped her feel more at ease, and she didn't have to worry about driving. Giving a slight acquiescing nod she held out her glass, then raised it to her lips and took an appreciative sip.

At some stage she was aware that the waiter returned and unobtrusively cleared the table, then suddenly he was gone.

'Shall we adjourn to the lounge?'

Sara glanced at the man seated opposite and made a deprecatory gesture with an idle hand. 'Why not?' She stood to her feet and moved across the deep-piled carpet with a floating weightless grace. Somewhere between the dining-room and the lounge she paused and turned slightly towards him. 'You haven't shown me the apartment,' she said pensively.

'How remiss of me,' Rafael drawled.

It was all quite beautiful, she decided as they progressed on a tour of inspection. There were three bedrooms, each with en suite facilities, a study, and a kitchen adjoined the dining-room.

'I suppose you send your laundry out,' she made the comment without conscious thought, then realised it must sound inane. Imagining him coping with such a mundane chore brought a smile to her lips.

'You find that amusing?'

Sara turned slightly and found him standing much closer than she thought. He exuded a sheer animal magnetism that stirred her senses, making her aware of him in a manner she found vaguely shocking. Her eyes widened as she looked at him, seeing something of the man behind the cynical sophisticated mask, and her lips parted softly as she recalled his solicitous regard for Ana. To be cherished and adored by a man must be a wonderful experience—something any woman would strive to achieve.

'Have I suddenly grown horns?'

The light mocking query disrupted her reverie, and she blinked at the subtle sensuality evident. For a moment she almost wanted to feel the strength of those arms enfold her to him in a mutually pleasurable embrace. His wide mouth seemed to have a fascination for her, and she found it impossible to glance away.

She stood mesmerised as he leant towards her and lowered his head, her body swaying slightly as anticipation of his touch overcame every conceivable caution.

Light as a butterfly his lips brushed hers, tracing the outline of her mouth with tantalising restraint before beginning an evocative trail along the edge of her jaw to tease an earlobe.

Sara gave an unconscious sigh as his hands curved over her shoulders and pulled her close, then his mouth moved back to close over hers in a kiss that wiped out every vestige of conscious thought. She was drowning, sinking lower and lower into a pool of such overwhelming warmth that she felt positively bewitched. A deep flame flared into pulsating life beneath his sensual mastery, and she gave a faint moan as his mouth left hers to seek the hollows at the base of her throat before moving lower to caress the gentle swell of her breasts.

Each separate nerve-end tingled alive with unbridled ardency, and she arched back against his encircling arm, delighting in the wicked ecstasy of his erotic tongue as it circled the delicate swelling bud that had somehow become exposed to his touch.

Then his mouth fastened over hers with shattering possession, hardening and demanding a response that sent shockwaves spiralling towards her brain, forcing reality upon her with such startling clarity that instinct alone brought a struggle for freedom.

Dear God, what was happening! 'Let me go,' Sara groaned the entreaty, her voice husky with self-loathing as he permitted her escape. She began to shake from sheer nervous reaction, and with an audible moan she swung away from him and attempted to restore a semblance of order to her clothing. Her fingers were all thumbs and she could hardly see for the stupid idiotic tears that clouded her vision.

Without a word he turned her round to face him and in a matter of seconds he had completed the task.

'Will you please take me home?'

Was that her voice? It sounded as if it belonged to someone else. Maybe the whole event had been a bad dream and any minute she would wake and find she was home in bed. However, the hand beneath her chin felt real enough, and so were the features of the man she was forced to look at.

'In less than forty-eight hours we will be man and wife.' Rafael declared with a deep tigerish growl. 'You could stay with me now without any qualms—in fact, I have an inclination to insist upon it.'

'No,' Sara whispered in palpable rejection, and her eyes seemed to resemble huge green pools as she silently begged him, 'Please!'

His fingers tightened immeasurably and his eyes darkened with glittering anger. 'You want my possession almost as much as my body clamours for its release.'

She could only look at him, and to her utter humiliation a solitary tear slowly spilled and ran warmly down to rest at the edge of her mouth.

'*Por Dios!*' he swore harshly. Icy control governed his movements as he pushed her from him, then without a word he crossed back into the lounge and caught up her briefcase.

Sara stood still, unable to move if her life depended on it.

'Don't hesitate, *querida*.' The cynical mockery evident in the drawled admonition held a warning she didn't attempt to ignore.

In the car she sat in miserable silence, enervated to a point where even conscious thought seemed an impossible task.

As soon as the Porsche drew to a halt at the kerb outside Selina's suburban flat Sara reached for the doorclasp with escape uppermost in her mind, only to find that the door was locked and wouldn't release.

'Will you please let me out?'

'In such a hurry, Sara?' Rafael countered mockingly.

'What do you want?' she asked tonelessly, trying to ignore the way her pulse began to quicken as he leaned towards her. She wanted to cry and scream for him not to touch her, yet every sensitive nerve-end tingled with an awareness that made a mockery of any words she might utter to the contrary. In the dim light she found it hard to discern his expression, and she gave an involuntary start as he trailed his fingers down her cheek.

'Margarita will arrange delivery of your wedding gown on Friday morning.'

'Thank you.' There was a politeness evident that owed much to her upbringing, and it brought forth a slight smile.

'How very—correct,' he said musingly.

'Is there anything else?' If only her heart would stop thumping! Surely he could hear its loud rapid beat?

'Tomás will drive both you and Selina to the church. Try not to be late, Sara. I don't want to be kept waiting.'

'Maybe I won't turn up,' she declared shakily. The mere thought of exchanging marriage vows with this hard devilish man was enough to make her want to run away and hide.

'I wouldn't advise it,' he drawled with dangerous softness, and she shuddered at the vague cruelty evident.

'I gave my word,' she managed quietly, and his mouth relaxed into a wry twist that bore scant resemblance to a smile.

'So you did. For Ana's sake, if not for mine, you will be there, eh?'

'She's a lovely little girl.'

'So you will give me a goodnight kiss that will last until we exchange both rings and vows in church.' At her obvious reticence he leaned closer and brought his mouth down to within an inch of hers. 'It isn't so difficult,' he teased gently. 'I seem to remember you showed little objection before.'

'Bastard!' Sara threw at him in a tortured whisper. 'I hate you!'

His deep chuckle was singularly lacking in humour. 'Ah, *querida*,' he drawled with damning infamy, 'whatever else you feel, it isn't *hate*.'

His mouth closed over hers with hard possessive force, destroying any illusion of gentleness, then with a gesture of self-disgust he thrust her away. 'Go inside, Sara, before I do something regrettable.'

It was all she needed to gear her into action, and in a flash she opened the door and slid out on to the pavement, not even bothering to give a backward glance as she ran up the path to the flat.

Rafael waited only until she had unlocked the door before turning the car in the opposite direction, and seconds later all she could see was the Porsche's blazing red tail-lights rapidly disappearing in the distance.

CHAPTER FIVE

As far as Sara was concerned the most pleasurable aspect of her wedding day was Ana's appreciation of it.

Viewed through the eyes of a child everything bore the appearance of fairy-tale perfection; herself as sole attendant attired in a replica of the bride's gown, her beloved papa looking so tall and darkly handsome beside the beautiful pale-haired girl he'd taken for his wife. Ana thought her heart would burst with sheer happiness from the excitement of it all.

The vows Sara exchanged emerged from her throat with a husky solemnity, and in spite of the afternoon heat she felt chilled to the bone as Rafael slid the wide platinum band on to her finger.

She was now Sara Savalje in name, and in a matter of hours she would become his in body. It was there in his eyes, the faint taunting smile he gave whenever she had the courage to meet his gaze.

Even Selina, dear fragile woman that she was, appeared to accept that Sara had been swept off her feet, and her regard for the two principal characters in the day's dismal charade could only be termed benign, doubtless assisted by the knowledge that she was to be restored to her beloved former home within days.

The buffet set out in the formal dining-room provided a splendid array of food for the twenty-odd guests who had returned by invitation to Rafael's elegant home.

Throughout it all Sara assumed the actions of an automaton, smiling and making polite conversation until she thought her face might crack with the effort.

'You've hardly eaten a mouthful,' Rafael drawled, and she spared him a darting glance under the guise of a smile.

'I'm not hungry.'

His teasing scrutiny held a thread of censure. 'A man likes a woman in his arms, not a bundle of skin and bone. Eat, *querida*. I won't have you fainting from lack of food.'

'I'm not likely to pass out on you,' Sara responded wryly, and she deliberately lifted her glass and sipped the excellent champagne.

'Too much more of that liquid ambrosia, and you'll hardly be responsible,' Rafael observed dryly, and she pulled a face at him.

'Are you saying I've had enough?'

His dark eyes narrowed thoughtfully. 'It is almost time for us to leave.'

'Where are we going?' For a moment she looked totally confused.

'We're spending the weekend at my apartment.' His voice held cynical amusement, and a series of emotions chased fleetingly across her expressive features.

'Clara will take you upstairs so that you can change. If you wish, Selina can accompany you.'

'For a last-minute mother-and-daughter talk? You're a few decades out of date if you think I need any enlightenment as to what's expected of me!'

His slight shrug was barely negligible. 'If I were to offer my help, no doubt you would refuse it.'

Sara's eyes flashed with sudden fire. 'You're darned right!'

'Easy, my sweet. Remember our bargain,' Rafael cautioned, and with a gesture of defiance she emptied her glass, then mindful of the presence of guests she proffered him a sweet smile before crossing to the waiting Clara.

In one of the upstairs guest rooms Sara surveyed the elegant dress reposing on a hanger suspended from the wardrobe door before turning towards the hovering servant. 'I can manage, thank you, Clara,' she indicated politely.

'If you're sure, Mrs Savalje.'

Sara experienced initial shock at the unexpected title, then with a reassuring nod she reached for the long zip fastening at the back of her dress. 'Really. I'll be down soon.'

A shiny dark head appeared beside Clara, quickly followed by a slight body attired in a cloud of cream silk. 'Can I help?'

Sara exchanged a quick smile with Clara before extending a beckoning hand to the little girl. 'You're just in time. I can't make up my mind what to wear. Come and help me decide.'

Ana beamed with delight as she carefully closed the door behind her. 'I helped Clara unpack the new clothes Papa ordered for you. They're all lovely, but there's a special one I like best of all. It's green, just like the colour of your eyes,' she revealed in a breathless rush as she crossed to the wide capacious wardrobe.

Sara recalled the dress, and gave a considering nod. It was suitable, and would go with her cream shoes and bag. 'If you like it that much, then I'll wear it.'

'Will you really?' Ana's excitement was endearing. 'Oh, Sara, you'll look smashing!' Her forehead creased as she suddenly became serious. 'Is it all right if I call you Sara?' She looked unsure and faintly apprehensive, and Sara bent down to catch hold of the little girl's hand.

'Sara is fine,' she reassured her gently.

'I'm glad Papa married you,' the tot confided with a burst of earnest affection. 'Even Grandmama approves.'

How nice for Grandmama! Sara decided wryly. Silvia Savalje doubtless saw her son through a mother's prejudiced eyes as a man who was God, king and several beneficent saints as well!

'Let's find that dress, shall we?' she suggested, and sparing Ana a quizzical glance she wrinkled her nose with sudden humour. 'If I take too long getting changed, your papa may take it into his head to come and find us, and I rather fancy making a grand entrance into the lounge without his splendid presence at my side.'

Ana's childish giggle was infectious, and Sara quickly slipped out of her wedding finery before selecting the dress in question from the wardrobe.

'It does look nice, doesn't it?'

The simple straight lines accented her slim figure, outlining slender curves, while the colour drew attention to her eyes and the mass of natural blonde hair framing her face with classic perfection.

'You look beautiful,' Ana told her with undisguised sincerity.

'Indeed she does.'

Sara felt her stomach muscles tighten at the sound

of that deep drawl, and she summoned forth a smile as she turned to face him.

'I'm almost ready,' she said evenly. 'I have only to freshen my make-up.'

'You must go downstairs again, Papa,' Ana bade him earnestly, catching hold of his hand as he strolled into the room, and he cast her an indulgent smile.

'But assuredly, *pequeña*. We will all go down together.'

'No, you must go first,' the little girl insisted, hurrying on to explain, 'Sara wants to make a grand entrance on her own.'

He nodded his head sagely, and spared Sara a slanting smile. 'Ah, I see. You wish to create an impact, eh?' He bent down and caught Ana up in his arms to place her slight frame high on his shoulders.

Ana's delighted laughter echoed from the hallway as Sara turned back to repair her lipstick. Solemn green eyes met her mirrored image, their steady gaze belying the nervous tattoo of her heartbeat as she drew a deep steadying breath. For one crazy moment she considered opening a nearby window and making an escape.

Dared she? She caught her lower lip between her teeth in pensive speculation as she pulled a brush through the length of her hair. Then a sigh of self-disgust left her lips as Selina's image rose before her, together with that of Ana, and with an unaccustomed gesture of anger she tossed the brush down on to the dressing-table, watching it bounce against the mirror before she turned and walked from the room.

'What kept you?'

Sara glanced up and met the studied watchfulness

in his intent gaze and smiled, tucking her hand into the curve of his arm in an attempt to present a loving façade. 'I considered leaping from the bedroom window,' she revealed with seeming sweetness in a voice low enough to reach only his ears.

'My, my,' Rafael drawled. 'Am I such an ogre that you would risk life and limb to escape me?'

'You're an arrogant devil,' she told him civilly, and his dark eyes mocked hers as he leant forward and kissed her—hard.

'Let's make our farewells, my darling wife. We have a short drive ahead of us, and I am an impatient husband.'

Sara's eyes widened in sudden pain, then she collected her wits and smiled—brilliantly, for the ensuing ten minutes it took to bid everyone goodnight and embrace first Ana and then Selina.

'You're insufferable!' The words burst forth from her lips the instant the powerful car left the driveway.

'Have you nothing more damning to say?'

'Yes—*damn* you! Damn your arrogant hide! How *dare* you kiss me like that in front of everyone!'

His brief slanting glance was hard in the darkness surrounding them. 'Are you suffering from injured pride?' His deep chuckle was strangely devoid of humour. '*Dios!*' The husky oath left his lips as a muted growl. 'It is infinitely pleasing to discover you prefer broken limbs to a night in my arms.'

Will you show me any consideration—a shred of tenderness? she wanted to scream. I don't want to be an object for any man's lust.

'I hate you!' she cried, sorely tried. 'You know that. What do you expect? That I should melt into a thousand pieces at the mere sight of you?'

'You're overwrought,' Rafael told her hardily. 'A glass of wine will help lessen your inhibitions.'

'I thought you didn't want me to pass out on you,' Sara evinced pithily.

'Neither do I want a scratching, spitting cat to do battle with,' he flung with harsh contempt.

'Oh, go to hell!'

'Aren't you afraid I might take you with me?'

The dangerous softness in his voice brought forth an impotent rage, and for the remaining miles she sat in icy silence until the Porsche growled to a halt in the underground car park of the Surfer's Paradise apartment block.

'Out, Sara.'

Blind stubborn temper kept her glued to her seat, and the next instant Rafael slid from behind the wheel to stride round the bonnet and yank open her door. Without a word he hauled her out from the car, slammed the door, then hoisted her over one powerful shoulder with as little effort as if she weighed no more than a child.

'Put me down!' She beat her fists against his broad back. 'You savage—*barbarian!*' She swayed with each step he took as she rained blows at any part of his body she could reach. 'Put me down, damn you!'

In the elevator she renewed her efforts, crying out as he caught one of her flailing hands in a painful grip. 'Ouch—that hurts!'

'Not half as much as you're going to hurt very soon,' he promised with deadly intent, and she renewed her efforts to break free with a frenzy that drew the breath from her body in deep painful gasps.

At the door of the apartment he extracted a key and inserted it into the lock, and within seconds the heavy door slammed shut at a backward kick from his foot.

'*Dios*, what a termagant!'

Sara felt her feet touch the floor, and she struggled against the hard grasp on her arms. 'What did you expect? A simpering, besotted *fool*?' Her eyes flashed green fire and she threw him a look of such utter loathing that his breath released in a long harsh sound, striking a chord of fear in her heart.

'How dare you *haul* me up here like a—a——' Words failed her.

'I have a debt to collect.' His icy drawl sent fear shivering along every separate nerve-end.

'And I'm it,' she spat furiously. 'A dispensable piece of merchandise, acquired for a specific purpose!'

'You protest so much, I am almost tempted to believe you've never had a lover,' Rafael brooded savagely.

'That you should be so unfortunate!'

One eyebrow slanted in mocking cynicism.

'Who wants an untutored innocent?' Sara demanded.

'Are you?'

Her eyes widened at the silky softness of his voice, and to her utter consternation she felt her lips tremble.

'Answer me.'

'What difference does it make?' she muttered, unable to look at him.

'You dare goad me to the very brink of brutality, then ask that?' He took hold of her chin and forced it high. 'Sweet Mother of God,' he swore huskily. 'Have you no conception of what you might invoke by such unbridled belligerence, child?'

'I'm not a——'

'Child? Very much one, I think,' Rafael declared dryly.

'I wish I was,' she cried bitterly.

'So that you might sleep alone?'

'I doubt you'll read me a bedtime story,' she retorted.

'You're a little old for The Three Bears, I think.'

'How about Red Riding Hood?'

'With little doubt as to whom is the wolf, eh?'

Sara glanced at him warily, 'I think I'd like a drink, if you don't mind?'

'Of course.' He appeared faintly amused, damn him! 'What would you prefer?'

'Anything,' she snapped perfunctorily.

'As long as it dulls the edges, hm?'

'I'd like to spend the next ten hours in an alcoholic haze,' she retaliated swiftly, watching his broad back with resentment as he crossed to the bar.

'Poor little girl,' Rafael mocked heartlessly, and she flashed him a venomous look that would have felled a lesser man.

'Drink this,' he commanded silkily some minutes later. 'It will help calm your nerves.'

Heaven knew she needed it! She felt as jumpy as a cat on hot bricks. Even just looking at him made her stomach muscles tighten into a painful knot.

'My nerves are fine,' she declared defiantly as she took the glass from his hand.

'Sit down, Sara,' he bade dryly. 'You're not going anywhere.'

'You'll see to that, won't you?' She didn't attempt to mask the angry bitterness in her voice, and she almost cried out at the inimical rage that darkened his features.

'You drive a man to the very brink of sanity,' Rafael reiterated harshly, coming to stand dangerously close. The glass was removed from her fingers, and even as she backed away his hands reached for her.

Sara wanted to scream out that she was sorry, to take back the words she had incautiously heaped on his head, but any plea she might have uttered remained unvoiced as his mouth fastened on hers with bruising force.

Oh God, she thought, nothing could be worse than this. In a moment of utter hopelessness she simply stopped fighting as the ravaging soul-destroying assault shattered the tenuous hold she had on her emotions.

His grasp altered subtly and he shifted her close to fit the muscular contours of his body, then one hand slid from her nape to capture her throat as his fingers trailed the delicate bones at the base of her neck, seeking hollows with a transient featherlight touch as his lips followed the same path.

A lambent warmth began somewhere deep inside and slowly spread through her veins until she was aware of every pulsing nerve centre. With a maestro's consummate skill he played each sensitive chord to a finely-tuned sensual pitch until she was filled with a deep aching need that only physical release could assuage.

She was floating, carried high on a tide of emotion that seemed to have no foreseeable conclusion, and she clung to the one solid entity in the swirling mist as passion hammered to be met.

Rafael's mouth was an erotic instrument that knew no bounds as every last vestige of clothing was removed. Sara closed her eyes and allowed her senses to take over, revelling in the dreamlike quality that seemed to invade her very spirit.

In her blissful nirvanic state she was unaware of Rafael's body shifting to trap hers until it was too late, and a scream left her throat at that first painful thrust, then she began beating him with her fists and twisted her head from side to side in an attempt to evade that hard mouth as it captured hers with a hungry passion.

The blood sang through her veins like quicksilver, spreading with wildfire speed until her very soul seemed caught up in his possession as slowly he began to move, creating a pulsating rhythmic pattern as old as time itself, urging her ever nearer to that previously unattained plateau of sensual ecstasy, until she cried out loud with the joy of it.

Everything developed a hazy rosy glow from which she never wanted to emerge, and she drifted aimlessly through the portals of sleep as the night hours passed, too lethargic and sated to move.

Something, or somebody, did, however, and she moved restlessly beneath the feathery touch that teased and tantalised her into wakefulness.

'Oh!'

'So, at last you awaken,' Rafael drawled, and his dark eyes became hooded and remote in their watchfulness.

Colour crept into her cheeks as she strove for normalcy. 'Is it very late?'

'In a hurry to get up, Sara?' he mocked, and a light musing smile softened his rugged features as her blush deepened.

'What about breakfast?' she ventured quickly, unable to meet those faintly teasing eyes as they raked her pink-faced confusion.

'I'm not hungry for food.'

Sara cast a desperate searching glance around the room and failed to catch sight of anything adequate that might cover her nudity. Where was her wrap? Then she remembered her neatly-packed overnight bag that must be exactly where she had left it the previous evening in the lounge.

'I'd like to shower,' she attempted civilly, and was unable to ignore him as he propped an elbow and leaned towards her.

'Later.' His lips touched her shoulder and slid inwards to the curve of her neck, beginning an evocative caress from which she sought to escape.

'Rafael—please!' She wriggled as his breath stirred a few tendrils of hair to tickle against her cheek.

'Shh, *querida*,' he said huskily. 'I have an aching need to possess you.'

'It's daylight,' she protested, shy beneath the degree of arousal evident in his dark gaze, and he chuckled at her reticence.

'Making love knows no timetable, my sweet. Besides, I want the pleasure of witnessing your response.'

Her eyes clouded as she pulled the sheet more firmly over her breasts, and she clutched the edges as if her life depended on securing that silken shroud. 'Please—I'd like to get out of bed.'

'Then do so,' he drawled lazily.

'How can I?' Sara wailed breathlessly, her eyes becoming haunted as she glimpsed his sardonic amusement.

'I've seen every inch of you,' he reminded her softly. 'There's no need to be shy.'

'You could at least turn your back,' she said unsteadily.

'Little goose,' he chided with a click of his tongue, then he bent down to retrieve something from the floor and tossed it across the bed to her. 'Cover yourself with my shirt if you must.'

With an inarticulate sound she slipped an arm through each sleeve, then she slid off from the bed clutching the front edges tightly together and all but ran from the room, conscious that his dark mocking eyes followed her frantic flight.

Her overnight bag stood beside a chair in the lounge, and she quickly extracted underwear and a sundress of white uncrushable synthetic silk, then headed towards the bathroom.

The antithesis of a functional room, it resembled something out of an elaborate film set, housing a shower cubicle, an oval plunge pool, as well as a spa pool. Floor-to-ceiling mirrors reflected gold marble fittings and the deep cream carpet.

Sara caught a brief sideways glance in the mirror, and a hysterical bubble of laughter rose to her lips. Rafael's shirt with its tail dipping down to touch the back of her knees appeared ludicrous on her slim form.

Water cascaded into the glass-walled cubicle at a finger's touch, and without further ado she carefully pinned her hair high on top of her head and stepped beneath the warm needle-spray.

With determined resolution she set about lathering every square inch of skin, giving the task her total absorption. Engaged with her ablutions, she failed to hear the faint sound of the door closing, and it was only when a slight noise alerted her attention that she looked up.

'You!' Her voice emerged as a scandalised screech. 'What are you doing here?'

Rafael calmly slid open the glass door and stepped into the shower cubicle. 'My turn, I think,' he drawled, and reaching out he took the soap from her nerveless fingers.

'Do you mind?' Sara bit angrily. 'I haven't finished!'

He was much too close, and she moved further back away from him.

'Do my back, *niña*.' The lazy direction brought all her latent anger to the fore.

'I will not!' she spluttered in helpless rage, and his soft chuckle was the living end. Without thought she lashed out at him, aiming her fists with wild abandon at any part of his muscular frame she could reach.

'My, my,' Rafael drawled lazily, fielding her flailing fists with an ease that was galling. 'What a little spitfire!'

'Let me go!' Her whole body quivered with rage as she endeavoured to pull free of him. Her eyes seared his, then widened as they caught the direction of his attention. With a reflex action she folded her arms across her heaving bosom. 'Don't!' The single entreaty left her lips as he reached for her, and her struggle to elude him fast became a pitiful gesture.

His mouth as it fastened on hers was warm and strangely gentle, giving the illusion that she could have withdrawn at any time, yet it was she who clung after those first few seconds, her body moving close to his as if it had a will of its own, and the warm fire that kindled low in her loins spread to encompass her whole being until she was mindless to all else but the need to be fulfilled.

Where there had been a cascade of water there

now was none, and she stood in mesmerised fascination as Rafael reached for a towel, and proceeded to dry her with slow gentle movements.

His lips parted in a slow sensual smile as he took in her bemused bewilderment, then his head lowered and he sought the delicate pulse throbbing at the base of her throat.

Sara caught her breath as a shaft of pure physical pain exploded deep inside her at the downward path of his mouth, and she gave a moan as he found a rosy peak, causing such exquisite pain she found it difficult not to cry out. Not content, he crossed the valley between each breast to render a similar treatment, making her plead for him to desist, and when he failed to take heed she grabbed hold of a handful of his hair.

'Damn you!' she cried as her whole body became one delicious tingling ache. His eyes searched his, seeing the latent slumbering passion evident as his mouth closed hungrily over hers.

'Put your arms round my neck.'

Sara's eyes widened slowly and she gazed at him with a total lack of comprehension. 'Rafael?'

'Do as I say, *querida*, hm?' he bade softly.

Her obedience was rewarded with a lingering kiss, then she was lifted high as he carried her out into the bedroom, and at the sight of that large bed with its tossed and crumpled covering she hid her head against his throat, and felt rather than heard his low tigerish chuckle.

His virile masculinity was a potent force, and the silent shake of her head was pitifully negligible as he laid her down on the bed.

With slow tactile movements he alternatively teased and caressed every square inch of her pliant soft flesh, his mouth following the path as his hands began an evocative seeking exploration that brought the ultimate delight in sensual pleasure. Then, and only then, did his body slide to cover hers, and his name escaped her lips on more than one occasion as the wild physical rapture reached its peak.

Afterwards she lay silent and still, too enervated to move. The realisation of what she had become beneath his sensual mastery was something which filled her with bitter shame. How was it possible to react in such a wanton fashion to a man she both hated and despised? Wanting to be little more than a block of ice in his arms, she had become a raging volcano!

'If you stay there much longer, I shall be tempted further,' Rafael's voice drawled as he propped his head on an elbow and leaned towards her recumbent form.

'You don't observe the niceties in any sphere, do you?' Sara said bleakly. 'You take without asking, and with careless disregard.'

'Is that what you think?' His voice hardened imperceptibly, a fact which she chose to ignore.

With withering contempt she turned to meet his darkening gaze. 'How often do you intend using me?'

For one frightening moment she thought he meant to strike her, then his eyes became hooded and his mouth twisted into a mocking smile.

'Wherever and whenever I please.'

'Doesn't it matter that I hate you?'

'Ah, *querida*, I love the way you hate,' he taunted softly, and with a swiftness that surprised her she struck out at him, connecting a stinging blow to his jaw.

'Little vixen!' Rafael growled, and catching hold of her wrist he pinned it above her head. 'You believe yourself to be mistreated, eh? Maybe I should show you just how gentle I've been up until now.' His hawk-like gaze assumed frightening implacability as he leaned over her, then his mouth covered hers with bruising force, ravaging its softness until her lip split beneath his savagery. Without any preliminaries he effected a deep wounding aggression that was equally a rape of the mind as well as of the soul.

Then with one powerful thrust he moved from the bed and stood to his feet. Halfway across the room he turned to tell her hardily, 'Now you know the difference.'

CHAPTER SIX

LIKE a wounded animal all Sara wanted to do was run and hide, and for a few wild seconds she contemplated doing just that, then common sense prevailed. It wouldn't matter where she escaped to, Rafael would seek her out. He was that sort of man. For reasons of expediency they were inextricably bound together, and in a clash of wills he would ensure he emerged the victor. Her clenched fists pounded the pillow in a burst of frustrated rage. Damn him! Damn, damn, *damn*! He was nothing less than an unfeeling, devilish *brute*!

'Are you going to stay there and sulk all day?'

Her head swung round at the sound of that deep mocking drawl, and she lifted a hand to push aside the tumbled curtain of hair that partially concealed her face. The mere sight of him created goosebumps in the most unlikely places, and it seemed as if all her nerve-ends rose up in defence of the powerful charisma he projected. It was sheer animal magnetism at its most deadly, she conceded ruefully, and at that moment she didn't know who she hated more—Rafael, for the response he managed to evoke, or the dictates of her own traitorous body.

'I'd like to kill you.' Her voice sounded clear and strangely matter-of-fact.

'You're like a spitting bundle of feline fur,' Rafael observed dryly, and his gaze was brief and glittering as it rested momentarily on her before he crossed to the wardrobe and extracted pants and a shirt.

'I wish I was,' she hinted darkly. 'I'd mark you for life!'

'I already bear several scars at your expense.'

He turned, and Sara saw with shocked disbelief a number of long red scratches running at differing angles down his back. There could be no doubt about the cause of their infliction, and she felt sickened that her behaviour in his arms had been so degradingly animalistic.

Rafael watched the tide of colour flood her cheeks, then recede to leave a haunting pallor. 'Do you feel better now?'

'It's disgusting!' she said shakily, and glimpsed one eyebrow slant in cynical amusement.

'Most women would give almost anything to be able to lose themselves so totally in the sexual act.'

'It's a physical lust, nothing more.'

'Not two spirits merging as one, without rehearsal, yet in perfect accord?'

His words sent shivers spiralling down the length of her body. It *had* been like that, a wild euphoric pulsating mixture of emotions interwoven with such fateful intricacy it was almost possible to believe they had known each other in a previous existence.

'You're very lucid so early in the morning.'

Rafael buttoned his shirt and pulled snug-fitting trousers over his lean hips. 'I'll make some coffee.'

Sara ran a bath and soaked as long as she dared, then towelled herself dry and dressed without haste, choosing a slim-skirted sundress split to mid-thigh with a strapless blouson top in a vibrant shade of blue. Her skin glowed with good health, its texture silky smooth and flawless, and several minutes of vigorous stroking with the brush restored her hair to its accustomed style.

'Orange juice?'

Sara moved towards the table and took a nearby chair. 'And coffee,' she accepted, and incurred a swift slanting glance.

'No toast? Eggs?'

'I don't feel hungry.' She sipped the fresh orange juice with delectable enjoyment.

'You should eat.'

'Why?'

'Breakfast is the most important meal of the day.'

'Don't play the heavy husband, Rafael. I'm not in the mood.'

His lips curved into a faint teasing smile. 'What are you in the mood for, *pequeña?*'

'Getting out of this apartment.'

'And out of my exclusive company, hm?'

'You said it,' she answered tritely, and he laughed.

'Poor Sara,' he mocked. 'Am I so hateful?'

'Yes,' she responded simply, and met his dark gaze unwaveringly, glimpsing cruelty and an element of ruthless implacability in his arrogant features.

'You see me as an unprincipled brute far removed from the adored father my daughter knows me to be, eh?' His teeth gleamed white as he openly taunted her.

'Ana is very much loved,' Sara said evenly.

'And you, of course, are not?'

The breath caught in her throat at that silky query, momentarily robbing her of the power to speak. Even the thought of being loved by such a man was enough to disrupt her senses, and she swallowed compulsively. 'Selina cares for me,' she managed quietly, and saw his lips twist into a cynical smile.

'Ah, yes. Likewise your regard for her is unquestionable.'

'I wouldn't be here if it wasn't.'

With calm movements Rafael drained his cup, then stood to his feet. 'Let's go.'

Sara slipped out of her chair and regarded him warily. 'I'll clear the table and take care of the dishes.' She began stacking plates together with efficiency, only to be forestalled.

'Leave them. Pilar will take care of it.'

A frown creased her forehead. 'Pilar?'

'The apartment is serviced, Sara,' he told her in clipped tones, and she gave a careless shrug.

'In that case, I'll get my bag.'

On reflection, it wasn't the most carefree day Sara had ever spent, for although Rafael proved an urbane companion, she was supremely conscious of his every move. All her senses seemed tuned to the finest degree, and she found it was galling that he should affect her to the extent he did.

Inevitably the daylight hours dwindled into darkness, and with the night came a further onslaught to her senses as Rafael permitted no reprieve from his lovemaking. At first she fought like one possessed, and only succeeded in arousing his wrath, so in the end it was she who suffered, and she wept bitter tears at the unkind hand of fate in linking her with such a man.

On Sunday morning they rose late, and after a leisurely breakfast Rafael told Sara to collect swim-wear and a towel.

'Where are we going?' she queried idly.

'Do you care?'

She swallowed the sudden lump that rose in her

throat at his mocking cynicism. 'I was just curious, that's all.'

He regarded her silently for several interminable seconds, then he said quietly, 'I thought we'd drive up to Toowoomba for the day. We can have lunch along the way, or buy whatever is necessary and picnic somewhere.' He smiled, a rare genuine smile that quite transformed his harsh features. 'I have a fancy to sit on the grass and share a bottle of fine wine with you, some fresh-baked bread rolls, chicken, and a rare cheese. We could finish up with fresh fruit, then walk it off. Does the idea hold any appeal?'

It did, and she said as much, even going so far as to offer him a shy smile in return. 'Where will we swim?'

'A swimming pool,' he told her, slanting her a faintly mocking glance. 'I don't fancy having to vie for your attention.'

A puzzled frown creased her forehead. 'In what way?'

His teeth gleamed white as he reached out and tilted her chin. 'In a bikini you're far too alluring a figure, my sweet,' he revealed wryly. 'Especially those two minuscule scraps of silk you deem an adequate covering.'

Sudden comprehension brought a smile to her lips, and her eyes gleamed with wicked humour. 'That was borrowed. My own is far less revealing,' she assured him, and her stomach turned a rapid somersault as he bent his head to hers.

'I'm relieved to hear it,' he murmured the instant before he bent to bestow a brief bruising kiss on her lips.

Toowoomba lay a few hundred kilometres west of

Now you can enjoy all 12 latest Mills & Boon Romances every month. As a subscriber to our Reader Service, you'll receive all our new titles, delivered to your doorstep– postage and packing Free. There's no commitment–you can change your mind about subscribing at any time, but the 12 free books are yours to keep.

Take Twelve Books FREE!

That's right! Return the coupon now and your first parcel of books is absolutely Free. There are lots of other advantages– no hidden extra charges, a free monthly Newsletter, and our famous friendly service–'phone our editor Susan Welland now on 01-684 2141 if you have any queries.

You have nothing to lose–and a whole new world of Romance to gain. Fill in and post the coupon today–and send no money!

Brisbane high on a plateau and was known for its picturesque gardens and many parks. Rafael proved an informative guide, and as the day progressed Sara found herself becoming more and more relaxed in his company.

On their return to the inner island mansion they were subjected to an enthusiastic greeting from Ana, and as a special concession the little girl was permitted an extra hour's grace before being escorted to bed.

During the following few days Sara concentrated most of her energies on cementing a firm friendship with Rafael's daughter. Not that it required much effort, for Ana was a delightful, well-adjusted child whose uncomplicated acceptance of her father's remarriage could only be regarded as admirable. Silvia Savalje, Ana's grandmama, proved to be a friendly, if elusive soul, serving a seemingly endless number of fund-raising charities, so that Sara rarely saw her other than at mealtimes.

It was during breakfast on Thursday morning that Rafael informed her that they were to dine out that evening, and Sara drove to the boutique where Selina worked and enlisted her assistance in choosing an appropriate gown.

At seven she was ready, unsure whether to be pleased or apprehensive at the prospect of the evening ahead.

'You look very charming.'

Sara made a slow twirl and inclined her head in mocking acceptance. 'Thank you. Selina helped me select it.' In soft floating cream chiffon, it had a deceptive plunging neckline that could be adjusted to be daringly revealing, or, with the aid of a clip, modestly demure. The skirt was a mass of pin-pleats that curled up at the threadbound hem, and there was an elegant matching jacket. Her only jewellery was a small tear-drop diamond on a slender gold chain with which she wore matching earstuds. An elegant evening clutch-purse and high-heeled strappy sandals completed the outfit.

'If you're ready, we'll leave,' Rafael indicated as he pulled back the cuff of his immaculate dark jacket and determined the time. He looked the epitome of male sophistication, his well-muscled frame expensively sheathed in an elegantly-cut dinner suit that did little to reduce the raw masculinity he emanated, and she suddenly wished the evening over and done with. Dinner parties, even large charity affairs such as the one they were due to attend, had never bothered her before, but tonight she felt strangely ill at ease.

'I promised Ana I would look in on her so that she could see my new dress,' Sara said quietly, and he slanted her a sardonic glance.

'You seem to have become attached to my daughter.'

'She's a very affectionate little girl,' Sara opined quietly. 'Of whom it would be difficult not to become fond.'

'Unlike her father, eh?'

'You said it,' she responded with intended sarcasm, and he gave a husky chuckle.

'Let's go, *querida*. I'm not in the mood for a verbal battle.'

'Strange—you usually enjoy them.'

'Careful, Sara,' he drawled. 'The fuse to my temper isn't immeasurable.'

'That's the understatement of the year,' she

declared, shooting him a wry glance as she moved towards the door. His cynical mockery did little to aid her composure, and she walked in silence at his side to Ana's bedroom at the opposite end of the hallway.

'Oh, Sara,' the little girl began ecstatically, 'you look beautiful!' Her smile became a wide grin and her dark eyes sparkled as she glanced towards Rafael. 'Doesn't she, Papa?'

'Indeed she does,' he agreed tolerantly, and as if to give credence to their supposed state of wedded bliss he placed an arm around Sara's shoulders and pulled her close in to his side, then he brushed his lips against her temple in a lingering gesture of affection.

Sara suffered his touch with a feeling of inner rage. How dared he subject her to such a blatant display? Offering him a singularly sweet smile she moved out of his grasp to sit on the edge of Ana's bed, then queried gently, 'Would you like a bedtime story, or has Clara already read you one?'

'Well,' the little imp began irrepressibly, 'Clara has, but I'd love you to tell me another.' She smoothed the sheet and folded her hands, then sent her father a beguiling smile. 'Do you mind, Papa?'

His compelling features assumed an expression of humorous resignation, and he leant forward to ruffle her hair. 'Why should I mind, *niña?*'

The child's answering smile made Sara catch her breath, and not for the first time she had difficulty reconciling this devoted loving father with the tyrannical devil she knew him to be.

'Tell me about some of the funny things some of your pupils have done,' Ana besought her earnestly, and with an unfeigned laugh Sara did just that, relating an incident that brought forth a series of delighted giggles from the little girl.

'Oh, Sara, did that really happen? You're not just making it up?'

Sara raised her right hand in solemn acquiescence. 'I swear it's the truth.'

Rafael stood negligently at ease, his expression one of amused indulgence as he surveyed them both, then with a regretful smile he moved closer towards the bed and tucked in the covers. 'It's time for Sara and me to leave, *pequeña*.'

He bent down and brushed his lips against her cheek. 'Tomorrow we fly out to Nooroobunda. You will enjoy that, yes?'

Ana's eyes positively glowed with pleasure. 'Oh, Papa—I do love you.' She looked up at Sara and gave her a slow shy smile. 'And you, too, Sara. Now we're a real family,' she sighed contentedly, adding with the simplicity of the young, 'I'm sleepy now. Goodnight, Papa. Goodnight, Sara. Have a nice time.'

In the car Sara sat in contemplative silence, and she was hardly aware of where they were heading until Rafael eased the Porsche to a halt in a parking area adjacent one of the most exclusive restaurants in Surfer's Paradise. 'Oh, heavens!' she murmured, unaware she had actually voiced the words until Rafael turned sideways and slanted her a mocking smile.

'You find the prospect daunting?'

Her eyes were serious as they met his, and she said quietly, 'I haven't attended any social functions since my father's death. There was quite a lot of publicity at the time. Can you blame me if I feel reluctant?'

'I doubt anyone present will do or say anything untoward.'

She grimaced a trifle wryly as she reached for the door-clasp. 'That's supposed to make me feel better?' She slid out and stood on the pavement as he locked the car, then together they moved towards the main entrance several yards distant.

'You're my wife, Sara,' Rafael said brusquely. 'And as such you will be accorded respect.'

'Nothing will stop the curious from conjecturing the real reason behind our marriage,' she retorted with biting scepticism.

'Then we shall have to convince them otherwise,' he stated cynically, and she shot him a startled glance.

'Precisely how do you propose to do that?'

'By appearing to have eyes only for each other.' The mocking cynicism was evident in his drawling tone, and Sara had to restrain herself from lashing out at him.

'That will be difficult,' she snapped, only to hear his amused chuckle in response.

'All you have to do is smile,' he told her. 'And leave the rest to me.'

'That's what worries me,' Sara returned with saccharine sweetness, and it was all she could do not to wrench her hand from his grasp as they mounted the few steps to the restaurant's entrance.

'Rafael—darling!'

At the sound of that husky feminine voice Sara turned with intrigue to see if the owner matched up to the image projected, and had to concede that she did—more so, if that were possible, for the woman gliding towards them was perfection personified, from her elegant hairdo to the tip of her expensively-shod feet. Without doubt her wild-blue silk gown bore a top designer label.

'Renée,' Rafael acknowledged formally, and Sara had the strangest feeling he was masking irritation at her presence. 'Renée Laquet—Sara, my wife.' The last two words were added deliberately, and as if to give them emphasis he lifted Sara's hand to his lips, kissing each finger in turn with lingering slowness, his eyes dark with an implied intimacy that made Sara squirm with embarrassment.

'Really, Rafael,' Renée pouted breathlessly, 'you will have your little joke.' Her eyes searched his hungrily, with an avidness that was vaguely sickening, and Sara found herself almost holding her breath for his reply.

'Sara and I were married six days ago,' he revealed silkily, and for a brief second naked rage flared in the other woman's eyes, then it was dampened down to become a mocking glitter.

'You'll have to forgive me, Rafael,' she said brightly. 'I must have missed reading about it.'

'We chose to have a very quiet ceremony,' Rafael informed her, and Renée uttered a deprecatory laugh.

'Why, darling?' She allowed her brittle gaze to rake Sara from top to toe. 'She's really quite a pretty little thing.'

'Beautiful,' he corrected with assumed indolence, directing Sara a look of such warmth she almost reeled from the shock of it. 'If you'll excuse us, Renée?' His dismissal was unmistakable, and the other woman had little option but to stand aside.

'My, my,' Sara voiced quietly the instant they were out of earshot. 'You should have informed all your former girl-friends of our marriage. That particular one is devastated!'

'I am answerable to no woman, Sara,' Rafael told her dryly. 'Renée, especially.'

'No?' she arched with deliberate obtuseness. 'She certainly had me fooled!'

His glance was oblique. 'In my line of business I have a large number of acquaintances, of whom several are women. You would be advised to remember it.'

Sara contrived an innocent smile. 'Good heavens,' she exclaimed, her voice gently chiding, and her eyes widened with a seeming lack of guile. 'I don't require any explanations, *darling*.' The added endearment was deliberate and brought a faint narrowing of his dark eyes. 'After all, you *married* me, didn't you?'

'Careful, *querida*,' he warned. 'You're way out of your depth.'

'But you're my saviour, Rafael,' she pouted prettily. 'I have absolutely no doubts about your permitting me to drown.'

There was mockery evident in his dark slanting glance, even though amusement tinged his drawling response. 'You are a perverse little baggage, Sara. The waiter is about to escort us to our table,' he added. 'Perhaps you'd care to summon your most captivating smile for the benefit of any onlookers?'

'Of course, darling. Anything you say,' she said demurely.

Tables had been placed together to accommodate ten guests to each group, and it wasn't long before all the tables began to fill. Sara played her part to the hilt, deriving enjoyment from her husband's apparent devotion, all the while aware of Renée's close scrutiny of their every move. After a starter of seafood cocktail Sara sipped an excellent white wine while waiting for the consommé, and let her gaze wander idly round the crowded room.

There were several familiar faces, whose very presence indicated the dinner to be a very prestigious affair, and she was aware of a certain amount of speculation regarding her appearance in Rafael Savalje's company. No doubt before the evening was over they would all be informed of her new status. Some would be genuinely sincere, others sceptical when they learned of her liaison with Rafael. Nothing would halt the rumours that would ensue, no matter how convincing a part she played.

Music from a group of five musicians provided a pleasant background to the aimless chatter, and on a crazy impulse she touched Rafael's sleeve.

'Dance with me, darling?'

His smile was faintly teasing as he replaced his glass and stood to his feet. As they reached the dance floor Sara began to wonder at her sanity, for once in his arms she was assailed by a wild breathlessness she couldn't control.

The music was slow and dreamy, an ideal accompaniment to aid patrons' digestion, and for Sara it began to have a hypnotic effect. She fitted neatly into his arms, her head tucked beneath his chin as he led her slowly between the dancing couples. Her body seemed moulded against his, and she was achingly aware of every muscle in that strong taut frame. On impulse she raised her arms and clasped her hands about his neck, and she uttered an almost imperceptible sigh as he altered his hold to enfold her even closer.

'Do you want to go home?'

Sara lifted her head to meet his gaze, and was

unable to suppress the tingle of apprehension that feathered its way down her spine at the slumbering passion evident in those dark eyes. 'Really, Rafael,' she chided softly, encouraged by the presence of so many people. 'What will everyone think?'

'The obvious,' he slanted a trifle dryly. 'Does it bother you?'

'Not really.' Liar! An impertinent imp prompted her to taunt, 'I don't imagine it will please Renée if we leave.'

'Cat,' he said grimly. 'Remind me to take revenge for that remark.'

'How could you be so cruel?' she parried sweetly. 'The poor woman is utterly devastated by your rejection.'

'Witch! I wonder if you would be so brave if we were alone?'

'I doubt there's anything you could do that would surprise me.'

Rafael's eyes narrowed at the tinge of bitterness in her voice, then his lips brushed her temple and slid down to rest at the edge of her mouth.

'Don't.' It was a plea uttered in anger, and she felt his lips relax into a smile.

'You're not very convincing, *amada*,' he taunted gently, and she made a choking sound as a stream of invective rose to her lips.

'I hate you,' she whispered at last, then his mouth was on hers in a manner that branded her his possession, and in that moment she truly loathed him.

'You unspeakable fiend!' she muttered when she had time to catch her breath. 'How dare you humiliate me!' There was a shimmer of angry tears evident, making her eyes appear large green pools, and Rafael clicked his teeth in expressed regret.

'It wasn't my intention to humiliate you.'

'Dear God—*what*, then?'

'Sara,' he warned with dangerous softness, 'don't goad me too far, hm?'

'Take me back to the table,' she said wretchedly. 'Renée might appreciate caveman tactics, but I don't.'

'I could shake you until every bone in your body *rattles,*' he threatened, and she gave a compulsive sob.

'What else is new?' She struggled in an effort to escape, only to discover she was held prisoner by arms of steel.

'Be still, *pequeña*,' he bade implacably. 'You'll only succeed in hurting yourself.'

'What are a few more bruises?' she choked impotently, and heard his harsh sigh.

'If you don't stop this *instant*, I'll kiss you as never before, and then we will be the cynosure of all eyes.'

There was a dreaded finality in the warning, and all her instincts urged capitulation. Without a word she allowed him to lead her back to their table, and once seated she reached for her partly-filled glass in the hope that the wine might help to restore her composure.

Sara scarcely tasted the soup, and the main course could have been sawdust for all the notice she took as she forked morsels into her mouth. Rafael was dutifully solicitous, and to any onlooker he presented the image of a loving husband, playing the part to the hilt, so that it was all she could do not to throw something at him.

'You don't mind if I join you for coffee?'

Sara glanced up at the sound of that huskily-voiced query, and saw Renée slip into an empty seat opposite before there was an opportunity to accept or refuse.

'You're being very possessive, Rafael,' Renée declared with a faint moue as she withdrew cigarettes from her evening bag, and extracting one from the packet she placed it between her lips. 'Have you a light, darling? I seem to have left mine somewhere.'

With indolent ease Rafael delved a hand into his jacket and proffered a compact gold lighter, and Sara watched in idle fascination as the flame flared to ignite the slim tobacco tube.

'I've seen some property,' Renée began silkily after exhaling twin spirals of smoke, ignoring Sara as she directed her attention solely to Rafael. 'I'd value your opinion. Shall we say tomorrow?'

'Phone the office in the morning, and I'll arrange for one of my men to meet you at the site,' he concurred smoothly.

'I'd prefer you to attend to it personally, darling,' the woman insisted. 'After all, our association goes back a long way.'

'Unfortunately I'll be tied up for most of the day,' Rafael refused without regret. 'Jake Edwards is well qualified to assist you.'

'We could meet late afternoon,' Renée persisted, and Sara could only admire the other woma's sheer determination. 'Even share dinner,' she continued in sultry tones. 'It will be like old times.' Her smile was brilliant, and Sara found herself holding her breath for Rafael's reply.

'I'm taking Sara and Ana out to Nooroobunda for the weekend,' he informed her with inflexible politeness. 'We'll need to fly out by five in order to land safely before dusk.'

'I see.' Renée's eyes glittered with vengeful fury, and Sara experienced an instinctive feeling of fear at the other woman's antipathy. 'It can wait until next week when you're free. I'll ring you.' She stood to her feet in one fluid movement, and with a smile that nowhere near reached her eyes she turned and walked back to her table on the other side of the room.

'You certainly have a conquest there,' Sara remarked with a wry laugh, trying to tell herself she didn't care.

'Jealous, Sara?'

She met his penetrating gaze and forced herself to hold it, managing to effect a negligent shrug as she dismissed in even tones, 'Good heavens, no!'

'Of course not,' he agreed smoothly. 'Some more wine?'

'Why not?' She watched him fill her glass, then raised it in mocking salute. 'Here's to Renée, and all who went before her.'

'I think you've had enough,' Rafael told her.

'Oh, darling, *no*,' Sara disagreed with mock dismay. 'Why, it's only my third.'

'And last,' Rafael informed her dryly. 'Perhaps we'd better dance for a while before you touch any of that.'

'Such solicitude!' she remarked with a sigh. 'How fortunate I am to have you for a husband!'

Standing upright, he caught hold of her hand and pulled her to her feet, and among the dancing couples he held her firmly, his expression assuming wry humour as she moved close.

'Hm, it's heavenly being in your arms,' Sara murmured as a wily imp urged her on. 'Machismo— you have more than your share of it, Rafael Savalje.'

'And you, minx, are courting disaster if you persist with this ridiculous ploy.'

'Disaster? Ploy?' She feigned perplexity and offered him a stunning smile. 'Why, *darling*, whatever do you mean?'

'Remind me to beat you when we get home,' he drawled sardonically, and she fluttered her eyelashes and pressed a hand to her heart.

'Rafael, how could you? Am I to understand you'd strike a poor defenceless female?'

'Much more of this, *querida*, and I can promise you won't sit comfortably for a week.'

'My goodness,' she retorted in a voice suitable hushed with shock, 'I thought you were such a gentleman!'

'Believe me, I'm showing remarkable restraint.'

'I do admire impassioned temperance in a man,' Sara declared with considerable *sangfroid*, and heard his deep chuckle. 'And humour,' she continued wickedly. 'Such an admirable quality.'

'In a minute, I'll hoist you over my shoulder and carry you to the car,' he declared with exasperation, and she laughed.

'How—primitive, of you, Rafael!' Eyes green with devilish humour locked with a pair so dark they were almost black. 'Is that a threat, or a promise?'

'Stop playing games, *niña*,' he warned with silky detachment, 'or you might get more than you bargained for.'

'Renée obviously thinks you're something quite remarkable,' Sara persisted musingly. 'Strange—you don't do anything for me at all.'

For one infinitesimal second she thought he would explode, then without so much as a word he led her back to their table and collected her evening purse, bidding those present a polite goodnight before escorting her from the restaurant.

'Rafael, I hadn't finished my drink!' The protest had scarcely left her lips when he turned, and she almost froze at the icy anger etched on his rugged features.

They reached the car, and he unlocked the passenger door first, waiting until she was seated before moving round to slip in behind the wheel.

'I'm sorry,' Sara whispered in an abashed voice as the engine ignited with a powerful roar.

'So you shall be, by the time I've finished with you.'

His meaning was unmistakable, and she sat in miserable silence, mentally berating herself for the folly that led towards her own destruction.

It became apparent after five minutes that he intended heading for the penthouse suite, and within seconds Sara had her suspicions confirmed as the Porsche swept down into the underground car park.

'Out.'

'Rafael——'

'You can walk, or I can carry you,' he said brusquely. 'Either way, it's immaterial.'

'For God's sake, aren't you taking this a bit too far?' Desperation lent an edge to her voice, and she watched in fearful fascination as he got out and moved round to open her door.

'You may well need some celestial help before the night is over.' He leant down and unbuckled her safety belt, then he pulled her out to stand beside him.

As the elevator bore them swiftly upwards Sara spared him a quick glance, and then wished she hadn't, for the formidable implacability evident only succeeded in sending shivery fingers of fear scudding down the length of her spine.

'I shall hate you.' Brave words that escaped her lips the instant the front door to the suite closed behind them, and he uttered a harsh laugh.

'In your own words, Sara, "what else is new"?'

'Don't,' she pleaded desperately. 'Not like this.'

'Anyone would think I was about to commit rape, or worse.'

'Isn't that what you intend?'

'No.'

Sara swallowed painfully. 'Rafael——'

'Are you begging, Sara?' His eyes lanced through her as he swept her into his arms. 'I shall see that you plead for the merciful release only my possession can assuage.'

'That's barbaric,' she whispered shakily.

'Barbarian, brute, devil,' he shrugged cynically. 'Those are but a few of the names you'll throw at me.'

In the bedroom he permitted her to slide to her feet, then ignoring her protest he began to undress her, and when every last silky slip of underclothing was removed he started on his own.

Sara thought she had experienced every facet of his lovemaking, but what followed became a torture of the senses as he led her to the very brink of sensual ecstasy, invading every secret hollow until she moaned for physical release. Like a wild thing she threshed beneath his wandering mouth as it plundered a hitherto unknown path, and she cried out in shocked disbelief as he took liberties she hadn't imagined permissible. His possession, when it finally came, brought forth an explosion of such magnitude she wept from the sheer joy of it, and afterwards she lay spent in his arms, too enervated to do else but bury her head against his chest in mute surrender.

Sleep claimed her almost at once, and it seemed she had only just closed her eyes when she became aware of the tantalising touch of Rafael's lips teasing an exploratory path across the gentle swell of her breasts.

Slowly she turned towards him, feeling the slow-burning passion ignite and take fire as he led her with infinite gentleness to the peak of sensual fulfil-ment. Afterwards he slid from the bed and carried her to the bathroom, turning on the water in the shower, and beneath its warm cleansing spray they bathed together, then, dry, they dressed in their clothes and left the suite in the early dawn hours to drive steadily home.

CHAPTER SEVEN

NOOROOBUNDA lay several hundred kilometres south-east of Brisbane close to the New South Wales border. Commanding a small acreage in comparison to the larger adjoining spreads, it ran a fine beef herd and leased out the services of a few select stud bulls. Beneath the managerial hand of Bart Curtis it was an extremely successful venture, and one Rafael had acquired some seven years previously, Sara was informed as a sleek Lear jet transported them steadily eastward with maximum ease and comfort.

In the confines of the small cabin Sara was supremely conscious of Rafael, and after last night the mere sight of him was enough to put her into a state of confusion. Though she was unable to meet his gaze, there had nevertheless been one or two occasions during the flight when his faintly sardonic expression had brought a soft tinge of pink to her cheeks.

Damn him! There wasn't a hope in heaven she'd ever achieve his equal in sophisticated mastery—nor could she envisage the day when she would become used to accepting, let alone participating in, such unrestrained eroticism. Even the mere thought was enough to kindle the throbbing ache deep inside her, until fire ran through her veins making it difficult to concentrate. The fact that he was aware of his effect on her rankled terribly, and she thanked every patron saint she could name that Ana's presence would provide a necessary distraction during the next few days. The *nights* she would deal with as each one arose.

'We're almost there, Sara!'

Ana's excited voice broke into her thoughts, and summoning a smile she focused her attention beyond the little girl's directing finger.

Spread out beneath the rapidly descending aircraft could be seen an expanse of sparsely covered land, dry at the end of summer, with the hardy tussock grass and spinifex evident amidst mulga-scrub and spreading gums. A clearing denoted an airstrip, and scarcely before Sara was aware of it they were taxiing to a smooth halt at the end of the runway.

'Papa has cattle and horses,' Ana enthused as she unfastened her seatbelt. 'Can you ride, Sara?'

'It's a long time since I've been in a saddle,' she admitted with a smile. 'Perhaps if there's a quiet rather elderly mare available, I might be persuaded to give it a try.'

'Sometimes Papa lets me ride with him and Bart,' Ana revealed earnestly as she waited for Rafael to unlock the door and secure the steps. 'We don't dress up at all while we're here, and usually Bart cooks steaks on the barbecue outdoors.'

Sara followed Ana down the few steps and stood apart from Rafael as he retrieved their overnight bags from a nearby hatch, then she turned at the sound of an approaching vehicle and glimpsed a Land Rover in the distance.

'Here's Bart now,' Ana announced with an infectious grin, and she caught hold of Sara's hand as they moved clear of the plane. 'Oh, it's going to be a super weekend! I love coming here. So does Papa,' the little girl revealed earnestly. 'I think he'd like to live here all the time.'

Rafael in the role of rancher? It appeared so improbable that Sara almost burst into unrestrained laughter.

The Land Rover drew to a screeching halt amidst a swirl of dust, and a tall rangy man of indeterminate years swung out from behind the wheel to grasp Rafael's hand before turning to catch Ana up in a bearhug.

'How are you, angel?'

'This is Sara,' Ana said quickly. 'Isn't she pretty?'

The older man's eyes seemed to sum Sara up in a second, then his mouth curved into a wide smile of welcome. 'Indeed she is, young Ana. If you ask me, your papa is a very lucky man.' He extended his hand and Sara felt hers become engulfed within his large one. 'Into the Land Rover with you. I'll grab the luggage.'

Ana scrambled into the back, leaving Sara no other course but to slip into the front seat between the two men. Rafael draped an arm over the back of the seat, and she was conscious of the clean male smell of him as Bart sent the vehicle speeding swiftly along the track.

After a few kilometres they veered left, and Sara's eyes widened as they caught sight of neat white-painted fences bounding home paddocks whose green pasture obviously owed much to irrigation. Beyond remote-controlled gates poinciana trees vied with climbing clematis, and there was an abundance of frangipani and boronia to lend a glorious mass of colour to the long low-set house constructed in a pleasing mixture of rough-cast brick and white-painted timbers. Shrubs and carefully-tended native bushes lined the slow-sweeping gravelled driveway, and as the Land Rover slowed and turned in towards the rear entrance a swimming pool set in a large tiled courtyard came into view.

'Like it?'

Sara turned at the sound of that deep drawling query and met Rafael's level gaze. 'It's beautiful,' she said simply.

Ana scrambled out the instant the vehicle came to a halt, and Sara followed suit, accepting Rafael's light grasp at her elbow without demur.

There was evidence of contrived casual elegance inside the large sprawling house both in design and furnishings. Scatter rugs lay on a slate floor in the lounge, whose focal point was a wide stone fireplace set at one end of the room. Several cushioned cane chairs and settees were grouped around long glass-topped occasional tables, and there were expensive prints adorning the pale wood-panelled walls.

Insect screens covered windows and several glass sliding doors, and as Rafael led the way down a long central hall Sara glimpsed a large well-equipped kitchen, an adjoining dining-room, and counted four bedrooms, two bathrooms, as well as a games room.

'Bart and his wife have living quarters a mere stone's throw from the swimming pool,' Rafael told her indolently as they moved back into the lounge. He slanted her a faintly mocking glance. 'Joan has prepared salads to go with the steaks Bart is about to barbecue, and the meal should be ready in about half an hour. Meantime, perhaps you'd like a drink?'

'Thank you,' she acquiesced. 'Something long and cool would be nice.'

'Can we go riding tomorrow, Papa?'

'I don't see why not,' he declared tolerantly as he crossed to a nearby liquor cabinet. 'Orange or lemonade, *niña*?'

'Lemonade, please. Oh, look,' Ana cried with delight. 'Here's Algernon.'

Algernon? Sara tried to hide her amusement, then gave up as a chuckle left her lips at the sight of the small Sydney Silkie scratching frantically at the wide screen door.

'And Benjamin,' Ana added unnecessarily, for loping up to stand behind the little dog was a huge German shepherd, whose very size and stature made Sara shake her head in amused disbelief.

'They're friends?'

'Devoted to each other,' Rafael told her dryly as Ana walked over to release the catch on the door. 'There's a cat or two around somewhere, as well as a few galahs.'

'And some ducks and chickens and turkeys,' the little girl added, her voice ending in a delighted giggle as both dogs tried to outdo each other for her attention.

'A real menagerie,' her father concurred as Sara moved towards Ana and the two animals.

Properly introduced, they lolled on the floor, faces between their respective front paws, obviously at ease with the attention they were receiving.

Dinner was an informal meal eaten outdoors in the vicinity of the tiled rear courtyard, and was followed by excellent coffee during which the two men became so immersed in business that Sara decided her presence wouldn't be missed.

Quietly getting to her feet, she made her way indoors to the lounge where Ana was happily ensconced in a chair viewing television.

The little girl glanced up with a smile and beckoned for Sara to join her, and together they watched a lighthearted comedy series until eight-thirty, when Ana rose from her chair with a huge yawn.

'Golly, I'm tired. I think I'll go to bed.' She crossed to Sara and gave her a spontaneous hug. 'Goodnight. I'll see you in the morning.'

Sara closed her arms round the child and bent to kiss her cheek. 'Goodnight, poppet. I'll come by soon and tuck you in, if you like.'

'Yes, please,' Ana said quickly, then she turned and disappeared down the hallway.

Ten minutes later the little scrap was fighting sleep, her eyelids drooping as she lay in bed listening to a bedtime story, and after a few minutes Sara stood up quietly, switched off the bedside lamp, then she carefully left the room.

Halfway down the hall she encountered Rafael, and her nerves leapt in jangling discord at the sight of him.

'Ana is already asleep?'

'Yes.' She addressed the monosyllable to the second button of his shirt, then gave a startled gasp as her chin was caught between his thumb and fore-finger and lifted so that she had no option but to look at him.

'You've been studiously avoiding me, *querida*,' he drawled. 'Why?'

Sara suddenly had difficulty swallowing, and the tip of her tongue edged along her lower lip in a gesture of nervousness. 'You're imagining things.'

'No,' he said softly, and his eyes narrowed as her gaze appeared to centre at a point below his own. 'I won't entertain a fit of the sulks, Sara,' he delivered hardily. 'If you have something to say, at least have done with it.'

'I'm not sulking.' She tried to twist away from him, and failed miserably. 'If you must know, I have a headache, and I'm—tired.' It was nothing less than the truth. She felt emotionally drained, and her head wasn't the only part of her body that ached.

For a moment he regarded her in thoughtful silence, then he directed quietly, 'Go and slip into bed. I'll bring you something that will help you sleep.'

Sara didn't trust herself to speak, and with an inarticulate murmur she turned and fled.

In the large bedroom at the end of the hall she unpacked her overnight bag, then gathering up a nightgown and a few toiletries she made for the adjoining bathroom.

The warm water eased some of her nervous tension, and towelled dry and deliciously scented with sweet-smelling talc, she emerged into the bedroom, only to come to an abrupt halt at the sight of Rafael standing indolently at ease near the bed, glass in hand, his tall rugged frame outlined against the wall by the subdued light from a nearby lamp.

More than anything she wanted to run and hide, but there was nowhere she could go that he wouldn't follow, and moving one foot in front of the other she slowly crossed to the bed.

'You look all eyes,' Rafael said softly, coming to stand beside her. With unaccustomed gentleness he lifted the glass to her lips. 'Sip it slowly, Sara.'

She choked on the first mouthful, gasping as the fiery liquid caught at the back of her throat, and it was several minutes before she managed to regain her breath. 'My God—what is it?'

'Cognac,' he enlightened dryly. 'Potent, but excellent for calming the nerves. Have some more—it will help, I promise you.'

Sara shook her head in emphatic refusal. 'I'm fine—really,' she assured him, not quite meeting his gaze, and he chided softly.

'Oh, Sara, what a little liar you are!'

'I'm not,' she choked, sorely tried, and he chuckled, his eyes dark with wry humour.

'No? I'll venture your emotions are in such a state of confusion you find it impossible to think straight.'

Goaded, she flung, 'After last night, what do you expect?'

'Ah, now we have it,' he drawled mockingly, and she retaliated with asperity.

'You behaved like—like an *animal*!'

His eyes seemed to darken until they resembled polished onyx, then he said slowly, 'Never having been subjected to such uninhibited intimacies, you were bound to find the experience—illuminating,' he allowed wryly, and she was powerless to prevent the swift tide of colour that swept to her cheeks.

'I hated every minute of it!'

'It wasn't *hate* that made you respond so passionately in my arms.'

Oh God! The truth of what had happened between them rose to taunt her, and in utter despair she turned and ran, only to be brought to an abrupt halt as hard hands closed over her arms.

'Little fool! You're more child than woman. *Dios!*' Rafael swore as she began to struggle. 'A man is torn between spanking and loving you! Maybe I should do both, hm?'

Forced to meet his angry gaze, she whispered

fiercely, 'If you dare lay a hand on me, I swear I'll hate you for ever!'

'That's a long time, *querida*,' he gibed softly. 'Are you sure you could do it?'

'Stop it, Rafael!' Her voice was shaky with emotion, and she put up a token resistance as he pulled her close.

'I haven't so much as kissed you yet.' His lips brushed against her temple, then slid down towards her jaw to linger at the edge of her mouth before teasing a provocative trail to the hollows at the base of her throat. 'You're incredibly beautiful, do you know that?' he murmured lazily as he slid the straps of her nightgown down over her shoulders, and she gave a choking sob as his mouth began a slow descending path to the burgeoning swell of her breasts.

The instant he reached one rosy peak she felt a betraying tremor rake through her body, and as she pulled away she gave a gasp of pain as his teeth closed over the tender bud. Scarcely aware of what she was doing, she caught hold of his hair with both hands and pulled hard in an effort to make him desist, then stifled a sob as he began an erotic assault on that erogenous mount.

Almost in despair she tore her fingers through his hair, tugging at its thickness as she begged him to stop, then she beat her fists against his shoulders until the crazy ache inside her slowly radiated to her limbs to render them jelly-like and totally malleable.

At last Rafael lifted his head, and his mouth closed over hers in hungry possession, consuming, *punishing*; then becoming warm and probing and so disruptively sensual that she thought she would die from the sheer rapture of it.

With a husky laugh he swept her into his arms

and deposited her among the silky sheets. There was the rustling sound of clothing being discarded, then his hard-muscled body joined hers on the bed, and as he reached for her the tears that had gathered spilled over and ran down to rest near the lobe of each ear before welling and trickling slowly down the edge of her neck to soak the pillow.

Eventually he tasted them, and his tongue followed each salty patch with such lingering gentleness it only caused the onset of an unceasing flow, so that he groaned and buried his head between her breasts.

'You certainly choose your moment, *querida*,' Rafael derided huskily. 'How can a man make love to a woman who silently weeps in his arms?'

I want more than this, Sara wanted to cry out at him—more than just the physical slaking of sexual desire. I want you to want, need, *love* me—all of me. What I am, what I feel, the very soul of me. Not just my body, the flesh-and-bone shell you use as a vessel, then discard without thought to the havoc you cause to the delicate fragile core that is my emotional heart. And even that is a traitor, at variance with what my head dictates. I should hate you for the way you wreak out the wanton in me. I see your devotion to Ana, the tenderness, the caring, and I could die just for the want of such a look, a touch; to know I held your heart as she holds yours.

'Sara?' His eyes were dark and perceptive, and far too discerning for her peace of mind.

'Don't, Rafael,' she begged shakily. 'Please—not tonight. I don't think I could bear it.'

For a long moment he just looked at her, then the edges of his mouth tugged his lips into a twisted smile. Slowly he levered his body away to lie beside her, then pulling the sheet over them both he cradled her close and tucked her head in beneath his chin. 'Go to sleep, child,' he directed quietly, and she felt his breath fan the tendrils of hair at her temple.

Slowly she began to relax, and gradually the lull of inertia claimed her limbs so that she closed her eyes and gave herself up to sweet somnolent oblivion.

'What are we going to do this morning, Papa?' Ana questioned as she plunged the last finger of toast into her boiled egg.

Sara sipped her coffee slowly, and idly watched Rafael fork the last morsel into his mouth from a plate that had contained steak, bacon and eggs. He looked thoroughly at ease and the antithesis of a high-powered city businessman. Nothing could tame the raw virility he projected, the sheer rugged maleness that seemed to exude from every nerve and fibre. Attired in faded levi's and a short-sleeved cotton shirt, he appeared at home with his surroundings, able to pit his skills on the land just as well as he directed his realty conglomerate.

'Bart is out saddling up the horses,' Rafael responded with a lazy smile.

'You're going riding? Will you take Sara and me?' Ana's eyes filled with sparkling anticipation as she turned towards Sara. 'You'll come, won't you, Sara?'

How could she refuse? 'I'd love to,' she accepted, not even thinking about the aching muscles such an exercise would provide. It was years since she had last ridden, but there was consolation in the fact that Rafael wouldn't consider any hard distance riding with Ana along.

'Lovely!' the little girl breathed with delight. 'It's going to be a fabulous weekend, I just know it!'

Sara had reservations about that particular remark, but she gave a cheerful smile and drained the last of her coffee. Rafael rose to his feet in one fluid movement, then tucked in his chair and moved towards the door, pausing to make a mocking salute before he disappeared outside.

'Come on, Sara. We'd better hurry,' Ana said anxiously. 'It's important to start out early so we get back before the midday heat.' She scrambled up from her chair. 'I'll go and change into jeans. You must, too. I hope you brought some?'

'I did,' Sara assured her with ease. 'Meet you in the lounge in five minutes, okay?'

In the bedroom she discarded her skirt and pulled on denim pants, slipped her feet into serviceable boots, then caught up a hat and moved back down the hall.

'Let's go, angel,' she said with a grin as Ana came forward to catch hold of her hand. The little girl's affection plucked at her heartstrings, and she felt an unaccustomed envy for the child's uncomplicated approach to life. If only the placing of her own emotions were so simple!

'Why did you call me "angel"?'

'Because you are,' Sara told her with a warm smile, and Ana appeared to assimilate that with considerable thought.

'You're awfully nice, Sara,' she said at last. 'I'm glad Papa married you. I prayed very hard that he would, 'cos I liked you so much.'

'Oh, Ana!' Sara felt the prick of tears and blinked rapidly before they had the chance to gather and spill over. 'Your papa is a very fortunate man to have you.'

'Both of us,' Ana corrected quietly and with apparent seriousness. 'We're a family now. You, Papa, and me.' She gave Sara's hand a squeeze. 'Maybe soon you'll have a baby, and that will really be nice. I'd love a brother, or a sister—or perhaps I might have both, one day.'

Oh, lord! What could she say to that? How could she cry out that she didn't want Rafael's child? An unbreakable link that would chain her to him for life. If there were love between them, their child would be a welcomed, cherished addition, but Rafael was capable of loving no woman, much less her!

'You're very quiet,' Ana commented with faint puzzlement. 'Have I said something wrong?'

'No, of course not,' Sara hastened in assurance, and she looked wildly for something to take the little girl's attention. 'Where are the stables?' She extended an arm towards a group of buildings a short distance to their right. 'Is that them over there?'

Successfully diverted, Ana launched into an explanation of all the farm buildings and their localities, so that before long they reached the stables where Rafael and Bart gave every appearance of patiently awaiting their arrival.

On reflection it was an enjoyable morning, for they rode several miles beyond the grazing paddocks towards the north boundary, and with Ana and Bart along it made being in Rafael's company all that much easier. Sara's mount was a placid mare whose pace rarely rose beyond a controlled gallop, and after the first few miles Sara found herself relaxing somewhat.

Rafael sat in the saddle with an ease born of long experience, and with a broad-brimmed hat worn low over his forehead he looked every inch the rancher. He was so much a man of many faces, Sara found herself just becoming accustomed to one, only to find he had assumed another.

The sun beat relentlessly down on them, warming and drying the air to a degree where sweat dampened their clothes, and Sara greeted with relief the men's decision to rest up for a while. There were trees ahead, and minutes later they slowed the horses to a canter before bringing them up beneath the shading branches.

'Bored?'

Sara glanced at Rafael as he helped her dismount. 'Why should I be?' she queried quietly, aware that Ana and Bart were just out of earshot.

'You seem —' he paused fractionally, then added a trifle wryly, 'contemplative.'

'It's rather difficult to conduct a conversation while riding. However, if that's what you require, then I'll do my best.'

'Sarcasm doesn't become you.'

'My apologies,' she proffered sweetly, and encountered his dark sardonic gaze.

'Sara, don't provide provocation, hm?'

'Why, Rafael darling, I wouldn't dream of it. Quite honestly, the thought never entered my head.'

'Are you two going to share this flask, or shall Ana and I finish it off?' Bart called teasingly, and Sara turned to join them, crossing to sit down beside Ana as she leant back against the tree-trunk.

'Hm, I needed that,' she said with pleasure as she sipped the cool liquid. A heat haze shimmered in the distance, and as she watched a swirl of dust rose from the ground and performed a strange and fascinating dance as the wind currents caught and played with it, then in a moment it was gone. It was hot, but not unbearably so, and despite the loneliness of the terrain there was a certain companionable solitude in being so far from civilisation. Out here there were no pressures, little awareness of time as such, and she didn't wonder Rafael chose to exchange the concrete and steel jungle for a slice of such peace and serenity whenever the opportunity arose.

'Have you gone to sleep, Sara?'

She slid her sunglasses up to rest on her hair and adjusted her wide-brimmed hat so that it rested at her nape. 'No, poppet,' she reassured Ana with a smile. 'Just drinking in the beauty of our surroundings.'

'It is nice out here, isn't it?' Ana declared with a satisfied grin. 'There's no noise, but if you listen hard you can almost hear things.'

Sara knew exactly what she meant. 'You like being with your father, don't you?' It was a statement, rather than a query, and Ana didn't rush to answer straight away.

'He's special,' she said simply.

Sara felt a lump rise in her throat and had difficulty in swallowing it. Part of her wanted to agree. Rafael Savalje was one of a kind.

'What are you two discussing with such seriousness?' the object of her thoughts pursued in drawling tones, and Ana broke into an undisguised chuckle.

'You, Papa.'

Rafael gave a wry smile. 'Indeed? Should I enquire why?'

'It would only give you a swelled head,' Sara declared. 'Right, Ana?'

'I said you were special,' the young girl revealed

with a ready smile. 'Sara agreed with me.'

His eyes gleamed with hidden amusement as he looked down at Sara. 'Two adoring females,' he commented quizzically. 'Such a boost to my ego!'

'Make the most of it,' Sara told him with a sweet smile, and he chuckled as he extended a hand in assistance.

'On your feet, both of you. We're heading back.'

The distance didn't seem so great on the way back to the house, and Sara was surprised when the farm buildings came into sight. Sweat ran in damp rivulets down the valley between her breasts, and she felt hot and sticky as they reached the home paddocks. A shower and a change of clothes were a necessity, and she said as much as she dismounted and handed the reins to Bart.

'Did you enjoy the ride?' Rafael's manager enquired, and she acquiesced with a smile.

'Very much.'

'So did I,' Ana enthused. 'It was great!'

'Such wholehearted enthusiasm,' Rafael remarked tolerantly. 'It appears the two women in my life are very easy to please.'

Sara fielded his teasing glance by addressing his manager with the query, 'Do you need a hand with the horses?'

'I'll help Bart,' said Rafael. 'You and Ana go and wash. Lunch will be ready soon.' His gaze was steady, his tone inflexible, and she directed him a stunning smile.

'In that case we'll go and make ourselves beautiful for you.'

Ana broke into a series of delighted giggles and skipped along beside Sara as they made their way towards the house.

'I think I'll run a bath,' Sara declared as they entered the lounge. She stretched her arms and felt the pull of several muscles. 'A nice hot soak with lots of bubbles will do wonders.'

'I'm going to have a shower, then I'll call over to see Rita,' the little girl declared.

'See you soon,' Sara bade as she disappeared into her room, then extracting fresh underwear, a skirt and top, she made for the bathroom, peeling off her blouse as she fitted the plug into the large bath, then she turned on the taps and added a liberal quantity of bath oil.

Soon there were clouds of steam filling the room, and slipping out of her jeans she stepped into the scented water, revelling in the foamy bubbles that rose almost to her chin.

Without thought to time she soaked unashamedly, adding more water as she pondered how much her life had changed over the past week.

So caught up in her reverie was she, Sara hardly registered the almost silent click of the door until a faint movement caught her eye, and she let out a scandalised cry as Rafael came into view.

'What are you doing here?'

With indolent ease he unbuttoned his shirt and shrugged it off, then reached for the buckle at his waist. 'I need permission to enter my own bathroom?' he enquired lazily as he stepped out of his levi's, and chuckled at her hastily averted gaze as he removed his briefs. 'So shy, Sara?'

'Don't you have any respect?' she demanded in a furious whisper, then she gave an incredulous gasp as he calmly stepped into the bath. 'You can't get in!'

His eyes twinkled with devilish humour. 'My dear Sara, I *am* in.'

'You're impossible!' she snapped furiously, and he laughed, a deep throaty sound that only increased her anger. Without thought she scooped up a handful of water and tossed it into his face.

'So you want to play, hm?' he growled huskily, and with galling ease he reached out and lifted her forward until her face was bare inches from his own.

Sara caught hold of his shoulders to steady herself, then let out a gasp as he kissed her, a brief bruising kiss that made her want to lash out at him.

'If you're all through with your ablutions, you can scrub my back,' he drawled, his eyes gleaming darkly at her impotent fury.

'Like hell!'

'Ah, *querida*.' he sighed mockingly. 'Where's your sense of humour?'

'I don't like being invaded when I take a bath,' she choked, sorely tried, and saw one eyebrow slant in cynical amusement.

'Not even when the invader is your husband?'

'Especially not you,' she declared vehemently.

'Poor Sara,' he mocked. 'Am I so hateful?'

She swallowed compulsively, then lifted a hand to push back a lock of hair that had fallen forward over her face. 'Let me go, Rafael.' A strange weakness assailed her limbs, and she pushed against his chest in an effort to put some distance between them.

'What is so terrible about sharing a bath with me, Sara?' he queried softly.

'Because it isn't decent,' she retorted swiftly, and coloured at his husky laughter.

'You are an innocent, aren't you?'

Her eyes sparked green fire as she demanded, 'Would you prefer me to be otherwise? Doubtless

Renée is conversant with every titillating trick in the book. Perhaps I should consult her as to your preferences in the bathroom, as well as the bedroom!'

There was a glimpse of terrible anger in his dark eyes, and for a moment she thought he might actually hit her, then he smiled—a savage ruthless twist of his lips that sent shivers down the length of her spine.

'I'm sorry,' she whispered, aghast at the hasty words she'd flung.

'So you should be,' he concurred silkily. 'Renée is a thousand light years away from you.'

'Is that a compliment or a condemnation?'

'I married you. Does that answer your question?'

Sara felt her lower lip tremble slightly. 'Don't play with me, Rafael,' she begged shakily. 'It's becoming more difficult with each passing day to compete with you.'

'Why try?' he queried sardonically. 'The outcome is a foregone conclusion, and you'll only succeed in tiring yourself in the process.'

In any battle he would always emerge the victor. It was useless trying to think otherwise. 'Please let me being go,' she entreated, unable to bear so close to him. In a moment her traitorous body would begin to respond, and that would never do. It was bad enough during the dark hours when she shared his bed.

'I can't persuade you to stay?'

All too easily, she thought sadly, and it took considerable strength to give a negative shake of her head. 'Ana might come looking for one of us,' she invented the excuse, and blushed at his mocking glance.

'My daughter has the good manners to knock on any closed door, and wait until she is instructed to enter—or otherwise.' He released her arms and smiled as she scrambled quickly from the bath. 'Run away, little mouse. Another time I won't allow you to escape so easily.'

Sara reached for a towel and wrapped its enveloping folds about her slim curves, then gathering up her clean clothes she turned to deliver a parting shot.

'One disadvantage in sharing a woman's bath, Rafael,' she issued sweetly. 'You'll come out smelling like a rose.'

'And no one will doubt the reason why,' he taunted softly, laughing as a blush coloured her face bright crimson.

After a light meal of cold meats and various salads together with freshly baked bread rolls, Ana pleaded for her father and Sara's company in a card game of their choice. Around mid-afternoon they changed into swimsuits and spent a leisurely hour in the pool, then lay out in the sun before donning their clothes and wandering around the farm buildings on a conducted tour of inspection.

Sara viewed the penned bulls with healthy respect, although idly grazing they looked anything but fierce. However, their solid stature was deceiving, and she was all too aware how quickly they could move when roused.

With Ana providing an adequate buffer, Sara felt quite able to tolerate Rafael's presence, and it was only after dinner when the little girl had bade them goodnight and gone to bed that she began to feel tense and ill at ease.

Pleading a desire to view a film on another channel didn't fool Rafael at all, and his deep husky laughter as he switched the set off prior to scooping her up from the chair into his arms only succeeded in bringing all her latent anger to the fore.

'Oh, is that all you can think about?' Sara flung waspishly as he strode down the hall towards their room.

'Would you prefer me to show indifference?' Rafael teased as he closed the door with a backward kick of his foot.

'You're a lusty animal,' she told him bitterly. 'Have you spared a thought to the end result?'

He moved towards the large bed, then paused to let her slip down to stand before him. Slowly he took her chin and tilted it. 'A child?' His eyes gleamed darkly as he held her gaze. 'Would you mind very much bearing my son, Sara?'

'Do I have a choice?' she cried emotively. 'Even Ana mentioned how nice it would be to have a brother or sister, or even one of each!' she ended chokingly, and Rafael's expression hardened fractionally.

'You share a natural empathy with children. Why not provide one or two of your own?'

'Why not a whole tribe?' she queried wildly. 'I'm young and healthy, and should serve as an adequate breeding machine.'

'Is that why you think I married you?' Rafael demanded hardily, and she uttered a harsh laugh.

'I *know* why you married me. I doubt I'll ever be able to forget it!'

'There are times,' he said pitilessly, 'when I could beat you within an inch of your life.'

'Why don't you? You've done everything else!' Dear God, what was wrong with her? She had to be insane to taunt him like this.

'Sara,' he warned dangerously, 'in a minute I'll render the spanking you so richly deserve.'

'Oh, for heaven's sake, let's go to bed,' she said wretchedly. 'I'm tired, I ache all over, and I'm so weary of fighting you.' Her voice cracked on the last few words, and her shoulders sagged in utter dejection.

'Then why try?'

'Because I can't seem to help myself,' she admitted miserably.

'Poor little girl, what a terrible life you lead, hm?'

'Don't tease me, Rafael,' she pleaded, and heard his faint sigh.

'What would you have me do with you, *querida*? Much as I enjoy breaking down your resistance, I grow weary of the battle you present at each and every turn.' His hands slid up her arms to cup her face, and she suddenly had difficulty in swallowing.

Without thought she ran the tip of her tongue over her lower lip, and glimpsed the faint narrowing of his eyes, then in an unbidden gesture she slowly reached up and wound her arms around his neck.

'What is this—an invitation?'

Pain momentarily clouded her eyes, and he caught sight of the faint trembling of her mouth, then his head descended as he crushed her close, moulding her slim curves to fit the hardness of his own as he took possession of her lips in a kiss that seemed to sear her very soul.

His lovemaking became an exquisite thing, tenderness mingling with strength and mastery as he brought her sensually alive, pacing her pleasure with his own until they reached the heights of ecstasy in one joyful explosion.

CHAPTER EIGHT

THEIR return to Surfer's Paradise brought a spate of social invitations from Rafael's associates that couldn't be ignored, and the first of these was accepted for the following Saturday evening.

A formal affair, Rafael had said wryly when taxed, and on discovering Renée Laquet was to be one of the guests Sara decided a new dress was definitely indicated.

After two days of fruitless searching she finally discovered the very thing. On the hanger it looked nothing out of the ordinary, but after being persuaded to try it on she had to agree it was exquisitely elegant. In black chiffon with a halter neckline, it gave the illusion of revealing more than it concealed, with a skirt that flowed from a fitted waist to swirl dreamily round her ankles. A fine black lacy stole completed the outfit, and Sara didn't even blink at the exorbitant price-tag.

It wasn't until Ana reminded her over lunch on Saturday that Sara remembered she'd given her word to accompany the little girl to a children's party during the afternoon, Tomás was to drive them to Coolangatta, and wait until the entertainment concluded before bringing them back in the late afternoon.

'I forgot to remind Papa,' Ana wailed.

'Never mind, poppet,' Sara smiled. 'We'll leave a message with Clara.'

The Mercedes sped down the Gold Coast Highway beneath Tomás' competent hands, and their arrival at the scene of the party was greeted with circumspection. It didn't take long for it to register that Sara was the cause!

'I told them I was bringing my mother,' Ana revealed in a whispered aside as they moved towards the hostess and her daughter at the far end of the lounge.

Not 'my *new* mother', simply 'my mother'. Sara felt unaccountably touched, and oddly protective of the young child at her side. They shared a warm relationship that had long since emerged from the tentative stage, and she was very much aware that Ana wanted her friends' approval—even perhaps their envy. In the very nicest way, Rafael's daughter was indulging in a little showing-off!

It was well after five o'clock by the time they could get away, and Ana settled into the back seat of the large car beside Sara, happily content that everything had gone according to plan.

'It was lovely, wasn't it?' the little girl sighed with satisfaction. 'You were the prettiest of all the mothers there.'

'That's the nicest compliment I've ever had,' Sara accepted with quiet sincerity. 'I'm honoured that you wanted me to come.'

'Didn't Amelia look funny with that hat on her head?' Ana dissolved into delicious giggles. 'And that awful Rodney spilling icecream into Susie's lap. She was ever so cross!'

It had been a typical children's party, Sara reflected with a smile—some delightful moments and a few disasters.

'Are you looking forward to tonight?'

Sara pulled a face and wrinkled her nose. 'Well,' she conceded hesitantly, 'your father has a lot of very influential friends, most of whom I have yet to meet.'

'You can't possibly feel shy?'

Sara managed a shamefaced grin. 'Indeed I am. This smiling exterior you see is nothing but a sham.'

'Papa will be there,' said Ana, as if Rafael's presence resolved everything.

'Yes, but I can hardly hang on to him all evening like a limpet,' Sara reasoned, and the young girl appeared to give the matter some thought before asking,

'Do you like to dance, Sara?'

'Yes,' she responded. 'Although it depends who I have for a partner.'

Tomás brought the Mercedes to a gentle halt in the wide sweeping driveway, and Sara was surprised to see Rafael emerge from the house to greet them.

'We're late, Papa,' Ana began at once. 'It wasn't Tomás' fault. The party went on for ages.'

He leant down and ruffled the smooth length of her hair. 'Did you enjoy yourself, *niña*?' he queried indulgently.

'Oh, *yes*! We had lots of fun, and everyone loved Sara.'

His dark gleaming glance held quizzical humour, and he placed an arm around each of them as they moved towards the front entrance. 'I'm sure they did, *pequeña*. Your grandmama is waiting anxiously in the lounge,' he added. 'You will tell me all about the party tomorrow, hm?'

'We'll trade,' Ana grinned, and Rafael laughed.

'It's a deal. Sara and I will see you before we leave.'

Sara mounted the stairs ahead of him, and in their bedroom she quickly gathered up fresh underwear and a wrap before making for the bathroom. 'I'll be as quick as I can.'

Ten minutes later she emerged exuding the delightful fragrance of *Arpège*, having indulged in the use of both soap and talc as well as a liberal spray of the matching perfume. Where Renée was concerned, one needed every defence available!

Slim-heeled sandals gave her added height, and she didn't bother with tights, or a bra for that matter, slipping the chiffon gown over her head and smoothing it into place as she fastened the zip. Now all she had to worry about was her hair and her make-up.

Fortunately she possessed a smooth clear skin which needed little artifice, but she took time to highlight her eyes with various toning shadow, mascara and the subtle use of eyeliner, before applying blusher and lipstick. Her hair she simply brushed, blessing its length and style for easy management.

'Ready,' she said with a satisfied smile as she swung round to face Rafael, and her eyes widened fractionally as they encountered his tall frame.

Attired in formal evening clothes, he almost took her breath away, and his lips twisted into the semblance of a smile as he moved towards her.

'You look beautiful.'

Sara swallowed hurriedly and prayed for composure. 'You cut a rather dashing figure yourself,' she answered evenly, and he gave a wry chuckle.

'Together we make a formidable pair, eh?'

'I can think of a more adequate superlative.'

'Have you no jewellery?' His eyes narrowed in thoughtful contemplation as he regarded her.

'Something around your neck, and just a touch at your ears. Wait there.' He turned abruptly and left the room before Sara could say so much as a word, to return within minutes with a slim velvet case in his hand. 'These will serve the purpose, I think.' He extracted a slim chain on which reposed a single diamond teardrop, placing it round her neck and fastening the catch, and she fingered it with a faint feeling of awe.

'It's perfect! Thank you for lending it to me.'

'I'll leave you to attach the earstuds,' he drawled enigmatically. 'Consider them a gift.'

'No,' Sara refused with regret. 'It's kind of you, but I couldn't accept them. Thank you,' she added politely, and saw his gaze narrow.

'They're yours, Sara. I insist.'

'You've already expended enough money on the Adams family,' she explained evenly.

'You're my wife,' he said with silky detachment. 'Accept whatever gifts I choose to offer you.'

'You've given me many things.'

'Not all of which you've welcomed, eh?'

Sara coloured beneath his gaze and glanced away. 'If we don't want to be late, we'd better leave.'

'The mistress of evasion,' he drawled sardonically, and she grimaced.

'Not always. You inevitably goad me into retaliating in a most unenviable fashion.'

'Poor Sara,' Rafael mocked gently. 'With those green eyes and such a temper, you should have been born with auburn hair.'

'I don't bleach my hair,' she retorted indignantly, and he caught hold of her elbow.

'I didn't suggest that you did. Let's go before we begin yet another argument.'

'It's all we ever do,' she said resentfully, and he slanted her a cynical glance.

'I can think of many occasions when we're in perfect accord.'

Sara didn't say a word all the way down to the car, and she sat in silence during the short drive to their hosts' residence, a large palatial home whose driveway was lined with expensive cars.

'Nervous?' asked Rafael.

'Should I be?'

'I shan't leave you, Sara,' Rafael declared dryly as they reached the impressive front entrance, and she turned slightly to slant him a wry glance.

'I'm no stranger to the social scene.'

'You're an enviable asset to any man,' he drawled, and she lifted an enquiring eyebrow.

'Good gracious—a compliment? How condescending of you!'

'Vixen,' he said in droll tones. 'Be thankful I can't immediately take you to task.'

'Since when did convention stop you, Rafael?' she returned sweetly, and heard his husky growl.

It was perhaps as well that the door opened at that precise moment and they were ushered inside. Sara was conscious of his hand at her elbow, the mere presence of him within touching distance, so close that she could smell the elusive tang of his aftershave mingling with the faint aroma of cleanliness he exuded, a teasing mixture of soap, the dressing he used to tame his well-groomed hair, and the fabric of his clothes. Combined with a latent animal magnetism, the overall effect caused havoc to her senses. Already each separate nerve-end seemed to quiver in anticipatory expectation, so that she longed for more than his casual touch. It was madness, she reproved silently—an insanity she had to conquer. The alternative was loving him, and that would never do.

During the ensuing hour she mingled at his side, meeting a number of people she had no clear recollection of, and whose names she was unable to recall less than five minutes after being introduced. Doubtless the second glass of superb sherry was to blame for her being so remiss, and she idly twirled the contents of the exquisitely cut crystal goblet, refraining from lifting it to her lips more often than once every ten minutes, then when dinner was announced she discreetly discarded it on to a nearby occasional table.

They were about to be seated when there was a minor disturbance in the adjoining doorway, and at once all eyes centred there as a stunning redhead stood poised for a few electrifying seconds before she moved slowly into the room wearing a look of such apparent remorse her performance most assuredly deserved an Oscar! Who else but Renée would engineer such a startling entrance? Sara thought wryly.

With the liquid fluidity of one of the feline species Renée walked gracefully to the head of the table, uttered a charming apology to one and all, then slipped into the only empty seat available—directly opposite Rafael.

The meal was a leisurely affair comprising no fewer than five courses, and throughout the ensuing two hours Sara was made increasingly aware of Renée's obvious preoccupation with Rafael—to the point whereby the voluptuous redhead excluded each and every other guest present.

To give him credit he provided no encouragement, in fact he was distant almost to the point of rudeness. However, Renée was made of resilient fibre—the hide of a rhinoceros didn't compare, Sara inwardly grimaced, marvelling at the other woman's persistence.

'We must have lunch one day soon, Sara,' Renée announced in the manner of one bestowing a great favour. Her smile was wide and fulsome, and about as genuine as the long silky mascaraed lashes that fringed her glittery golden eyes. 'I'll ring you.'

'Thank you,' Sara acknowledged, injecting just the right amount of revered awe into her voice. 'I'll look forward to it.'

'We have such a lot to talk about,' Renée murmured, then she uttered a tinkling laugh that ended with a pouting moue. 'How you managed to snare this gorgeous man, for instance. I've been trying for years to pin him down.'

Sara let her eyes widen in deliberate wonderment. 'My goodness! I managed without any effort at all.' She slid her gaze towards the subject of their discussion and proffered a singularly sweet smile. 'Didn't I, darling?'

Rafael's dark eyes lit with devilish amusement, and she watched as he caught her hand in his, lifting it to touch his lips against the sensitive cord at her wrist. 'I am totally enamoured, *querida*.' There was blatant sensuality in that liquid gaze, a warm intimacy evident that caused the room and its occupants to fade into shadowy insignificance. Sara couldn't tear her eyes from his, and with a soft laugh he leant forward and lightly brushed her lips with his own.

Everything that came after that seemed to evolve amidst a hazy glow. Somehow Sara managed to converse with her fellow guests, although on what topic she couldn't have said if her life depended on it!

'You're very quiet.'

Sara turned her head slightly and was unable to gain much from Rafael's drawling observance in the dim light of the car's interior. It was late and she was in a dreamy state of tiredness, the effects of good food and wine. 'I'm sleepy,' she explained, and heard his faint chuckle.

'Not too sleepy, I hope?'

'I shan't answer that,' she declared, too content at that moment to care what he might choose to think. Her lids lowered of their own volition and she dozed, becoming dimly aware that at some stage she appeared to be floating, then she heard Rafael's voice and felt his hands slip the clothes from her body.

'Sweet mother of heaven, did you wear nothing at all beneath this whispery creation?'

Sara slowly opened her eyes and glimpsed the familiar walls of their bedroom. 'We're home,' she said unnecessarily.

'In a few minutes you'll be in bed.'

'How nice,' she husked softly, reaching up to wind her arms around his neck. 'Are you going to kiss me, Rafael?'

'My, my,' he chuckled, doing just that. 'What a chameleon—from vixen to seductress!' He swept her on to the bed in one easy movement, then slid down to lie beside her.

His lovemaking had a teasing quality, a light gentleness that made her feel warm and infinitely cared for, so that afterwards she curled up against him to sleep in his arms with the trustfulness of a child.

Shortly after nine o'clock on Monday morning Sara picked up the phone and dialled Selina's boutique with the intention of inviting her mother out to lunch. It had been more than a week since they had last seen each other, and with Rafael not expected home until the evening and Ana in school, it seemed an ideal opportunity for them to meet.

'Think of somewhere madly expensive,' said Sara with a light laugh. 'I'll call for you at twelve.'

No sooner had she replaced the receiver than the phone rang again, and she picked it up and answered with sombre judiciousness, 'Savalje residence.' Tomás, or Clara, would have a fit, she thought without a shred of guilt.

'Mrs Savalje,' a bleak feminine voice demanded without any preliminaries.

Continuing the farce a step further, Sara queried with unctuous civility, 'May I ask who is calling?'

'Miss Laquet.'

Help! Renée certainly hadn't wasted much time! Sara covered the mouthpiece with one hand and counted to fifty—slowly. Then she placed the handpiece against her ear and ventured sweetly, 'Renée? How nice of you to call.' Liar, she discounted wryly. This was one conversation she could well do without.

'Let's cut the pleasantries, shall we?' the other woman declared without preamble. 'You may be young, but you're not stupid.'

'You have something to say, I take it,' said Sara, and heard Renée's sharp intake of breath.

'Rafael is mine, do you hear? *Mine*. Our relationship goes back years—*years!*' Her voice fairly crackled down the line with spite. 'I suppose you imagine you've got him wrapped round your little finger. Poor little girl,' she sneered vengefully. 'Rafael is anything but the faithful type. Why, only last week he met me for lunch.' She uttered a bitter laugh. 'Surprised, Sara? I'll give you another shock, shall I? He happens to be meeting me again today.' She paused fractionally, waiting for Sara's reaction, and when none was forthcoming, she continued slowly, 'Be at Fiorini's just after twelve, if you don't believe me.'

As if in a daze Sara said carefully, 'Rafael must entertain acquaintances over countless business lunches.'

'Don't be naïve, Sara!' Renée's voice rose sharply as she went on to reveal in scathing tones, 'Rafael is very much a man, sweetie, with a healthy sexual appetite.' Her laugh made Sara wince. 'But then I don't need to tell you that, do I?' She went on very softly, revealing dates, times and places of previous meetings, then ended in serious tones, 'The Surfer's penthouse suite is quite something, don't you agree? I thought you might have rearranged the furniture, but you haven't, have you, Sara?'

'Why should I?' Sara parried evenly. 'It's perfect as it is.'

'Fiorini's at twelve, Sara. Don't forget,' Renée declared harshly, then the line went dead.

Sara stood transfixed for several seconds, too numb to do anything other than stare sightlessly into space, then she stirred herself sufficiently to go upstairs.

Unable to settle to anything, she freshened her make-up, then went down to tell Clara that she'd be away for most of the day.

Without no particular purpose in mind she drove towards Brisbane and after parking the car in the inner city, she wandered aimlessly, browsing in shop windows. None of the displays registered, and she heard none of the street sounds abounding round her. There was only the insinuating discord of Renée's voice running through her brain playing and replaying her horrid revelations.

Torn as she was between the need to check out Renée's accusations and the instinctive desire to discount them, the latter won out, and it was almost twelve-thirty when she entered Fiorini's with Selina.

'What are you going to have, darling?'

Sara endeavoured to evince an interest in the menu. 'I'm not really hungry,' she said. 'Just a salad, I think.'

'I'm going to indulge in something more substantial,' Selina declared, ordering veal parmigiana, then when the waiter left she glanced at her daughter and smiled. 'You look—pensive. Is something bothering you?'

'No, of course not,' Sara responded quickly—too quickly. Oh, for heaven's sake, this would never do! She was a mass of nerves, and too afraid to cast an encompassing glance at the room's occupants for fear of having Renée's poisonous words confirmed.

After ten agonising minutes during which she didn't taste so much as a morsel, Sara let her eyes wander slowly round the room, forcing them to pause occasionally as if her interest was merely casual. Her surveillance was almost complete when a familiar head riveted her attention.

At first she didn't believe her eyes, but the proof was there. Sitting at a corner table on the far side of the room was Rafael, and seated opposite him was the stunningly beautiful Renée.

Anger rose like lava spuming up from a live volcano. Sara's eyes sparked fire even as her features froze into an expressionless mask.

'Would you mind very much if we left?'

Selina looked momentarily startled, then sensing something was amiss she spared the appetising veal a regretful glance and replaced her knife and fork down on to the plate. 'Not at all, darling. I'm not particularly hungry.' She cast her daughter a piercingly sweet smile and stood to her feet. 'Shall we go?'

Sara fumed during the entire time it took to reach her former home, hardly aware that her mother maintained a tactful silence, and her refusal to go inside for coffee was politely distant.

'Ring me when you get back to Surfer's, darling,' Selina bade with a trace of anxiety as she slipped from the passenger seat, and Sara gave a perfunctory nod.

Her actions behind the wheel were that of an automaton, and it appeared whichever patron saint looked down that day had her interest very much at heart, for she reached home without incident.

The large house seemed strangely empty without Ana's sparkling presence, and Sara paced the lounge for countless minutes trying to determine her next course of action.

She could, of course, ignore the whole thing and pretend it never happened. Alternatively, she could tax him with it. For all she knew, there was a perfectly logical reason for Rafael to be lunching with Renée. It could be purely business. A snort of derision escaped her lips. Business—*Renée?* The only business Renée Laquet had on her mind was Rafael!

Her mind seethed with numerous possibilities. It

could even be coincidence they happened to meet, and what more natural than to decide to share a meal? Sharing a meal didn't constitute sharing a bed.

Oh God! If only she were sure of him, she could laugh about the whole thing. He desired her, that much was certain—but love? Rafael loved no woman, and specially not *her*.

Resolution became determination not to spend fruitless hours in a state of mental turmoil. What she needed was something to take her mind off her inimical husband, and she could think of nothing better than a totally improbable shopping spree.

Suiting thought to action, Sara caught up her bag and left the house, then sliding in behind the wheel of the powerful Porsche she sent it purring down the driveway.

After parking the car on the Esplanade she made for the nearest boutique without any clear indication of what she might buy.

Three hours later the back seat of the Porsche was loaded with brightly-wrapped packages of various assorted sizes. It bothered her not a whit that she had spent a considerable amount of money. Rafael would get a shock when the bills began coming in. He was wealthy enough to afford anything she wanted, and if he chose to play around, then he could darned well pay!

'I trust you spent an interesting day?'

Sara tossed the car keys down on to a nearby coffee table and deposited her bag alongside them before crossing to accept the glass of sherry Rafael held out for her.

'Very,' she declared succinctly, lifting the glass to her lips and taking an appreciative sip before directing him a levelling stare. 'And you?'

His nod was slightly mocking. 'The usual.'

Indeed! Sweetly she persevered, 'Nothing untoward?'

'Busy. I'll be glad when this merger goes through.'

'The wheels of big business,' she shrugged lightly, moving away to stand several feet distant.

'I thought we might go away for a while,' Rafael suggested with musing indolence, and Sara gave a graceless shrug.

'Ana doesn't have her holidays until May. What arrangements do you have in mind?'

'I meant you and me,' he said wryly. 'A week, possibly ten days. How do you feel about Hawaii?'

'Hawaii is a very beautiful place.' Unconcern lent her the courage to suggest with impish disregard, 'After so much sunshine I personally prefer a contrast. Switzerland, perhaps? St Moritz is fashionable, and it's a few years since I tried my hand on the slopes.'

'You ski?'

'After a fashion,' she conceded. 'Do you?' She gave a humourless laugh. 'Oh, forgive me—skiing is doubtless one of your many talents. You're adept at most everything.' Including seeing another woman behind my back, she echoed silently.

'Your tongue is particularly sharp this evening. What bothers you, *querida*?'

That easing endearment did it. '*You* do!'

'Indeed?' Amusement lurked at the corners of his mouth. 'Have I neglected you in some way, perhaps?'

'Don't worry, I've more than made up for it,' Sara declared with unaccustomed belligerence, and his eyes narrowed in thoughtful speculation.

'Elaborate, *niña*.' It was a command she chose to ignore, refusing to be intimidated when his expression hardened. 'Sara?' The threat of anger made his voice silky-smooth, and she wondered at her temerity. There were definitely times when it paid to take the line of least resistance, but she was spoiling for a fight.

'Did you enjoy your luncheon date?'

For an infinitesimal second his eyes gleamed in sudden comprehension, then they became hooded as he lazily took a generous swallow of whisky. 'Are you jealous, *niña*, because I happened to lunch with someone other than you?'

'I couldn't care less who you lunch with—or dine with, for that matter,' she dismissed swiftly, and her lips took a bitter twist. 'You don't deny that you had a luncheon date with Renée?'

'Why should I?' Rafael countered smoothly. 'Her father is a valued business associate, and Renée has been dabbling in real estate quite successfully for the past five years.'

'No doubt due to your excellent advice.'

'She has consulted me on several ventures—yes.'

'My God!' Sara declared piously. 'I wouldn't put it past her to have developed an interest in property solely for the purpose of hiring your services. She'd be in your bed given the slightest opportunity.'

Rafael gave an imperceptible shrug, but she was all too aware that beneath half-lowered lids his eyes were dangerously alert. 'Don't make any accusations you can't substantiate, *niña*,' he drawled, and she flew into a temper at once.

'Stop using childish nicknames! It sounds endearing with someone of Ana's age, but I left the school-room years ago!'

'It's a pity you didn't achieve an enviable maturity to complement your status.'

Sara felt her voice rise in rage. 'You diabolical fiend—what's that supposed to mean? That I should condone your liaison with another woman?' Her eyes sparked green fire and her cheeks were alive with colour. 'If that's maturity, then I'll pass!'

His expression was deliberately enigmatic. 'A few minutes ago you stated you didn't care who I lunched or dined with.'

'Renée is different,' she muttered trenchantly, unable to meet his gaze.

'Whom you would prefer me not to see—in any capacity?'

'You're a married man,' she flung bitterly, and could have wept at the devilish cynicism she glimpsed in those dark eyes.

'Ah, I see,' Rafael mocked quietly. 'You were upset.'

'No—*yes,* damn you!' she choked. 'If you're going to have an affair, at least have the decency to do it discreetly!'

His faint chuckle was definitely quizzical. 'My dear Sara, we conduct a very satisfactory sexual relationship every night, and most often in the early morning hours as well. Where do you imagine I'd find the energy, let alone the inclination, to bed someone else on the side?'

'I'm sure you'd manage, given sufficient provocation.'

'Do you want my oath of fidelity?'

'As a salve to your conscience?' Sara parried. 'Only to continue innumerable clandestine meetings with the glamorous Renée—who, incidentally, couldn't give a fig for anyone other than herself.' She shook her head slowly from side to side. 'It never ceases to amaze me how blind men can be in the face of a beautiful woman.'

'The reason is fairly basic, wouldn't you agree?'

His drawling cynicism was the living end, and she erupted into angry speech.

'You—bastard!' Words tumbled from her lips in a torrent of loathing. 'I've already been given well-meaning advice about your—rakish reputation.'

'You're over-reacting, Sara.'

'Am I?' she queried sadly. 'I notice you don't bother denying it.'

His silence was enervating, then he offered hardily, 'Would you believe me if I did?'

She swallowed painfully, and her eyes didn't falter as they held his gaze. 'The evidence is stacked against you, Rafael.'

His eyes narrowed fractionally, and a muscle tensed along his jaw. 'What the hell are you talking about?'

Her gaze remained steady. 'Renée was quite lucid in her recount of every sordid detail. Dates, places— even time to the precise hour on occasion,' she revealed stoically, and saw his features tauten into an iron mask.

'That young woman has a lot to answer for,' he growled harshly.

'It takes two,' Sara reminded him bitterly.

'For the love of heaven!' Rafael swore emotively. 'My relationship with Renée was over long before you left the schoolroom.' His eyes seemed to pierce right through to her very soul. 'The Renées of this world are like birds in a gilded cage—constantly in need of attention and admiration. They are as false as their existence,' he added pitilessly.

'How sad,' Sara declared with wry cynicism. 'My heart bleeds for her.'

'Go and get changed,' Rafael ordered brusquely. 'We'll go somewhere for dinner.'

A stray lock of hair fell forward, and she brushed it back with an impatient gesture. 'I'd rather not, if you don't mind. I don't think I'd be very good company.'

'Nonsense. It will do you good.'

She gave him a baleful look. 'You ride roughshod over everyone, don't you?'

'I know a very good seafood restaurant where the food is superb,' he drawled. 'We could go on to a nightclub afterwards.'

'One of your favourite haunts?' she taunted, her glance derisory. 'And risk running into Renée? Thanks, but no, thanks.'

He straightened and moved towards her with an indolent grace, and she watched in idle fascination as he paused directly in front of her. 'Sara, do as you're told, hm?' He reached out a hand and brushed his fingers down her cheek in a strangely gentle gesture. 'I'd like to take you out so that we can enjoy a few hours together, with some excellent food, a good palatable wine. We could dance, or watch a floor show. Doesn't that have any appeal?' He leant forward and lightly brushed his lips over the top of her hair, then trailed them down to caress her temple.

It was a flagrant seduction, and against her will he felt her senses begin to stir at his potent magnetism. Oh God, would it always be like this? she moaned silently as his lips began a slow downwards trail over her cheekbone to the edge of her mouth. She could feel all her fine body hairs tingle in awareness, and without being aware of it she swayed towards him, her face lifting of its own volition for his kiss.

Rafael's mouth teased along her lower lip, tantalising with an evocative sensuality that set the blood pulsing warmly through her veins. She was melting, drifting way out of her depth, and with unashamed capitulation she clung to him, winding her arms up round his neck as her mouth opened beneath his like a flower to the morning sun.

There was hunger in his touch that met an answering response as the kiss deepened to a consuming passion that knew no bounds, and she gave a tiny moan of entreaty when he caught her up into his arms.

'Rafael—no!' The protest was half-hearted at best, and they both knew it.

'Sara—*yes*,' he mocked gently, and his dark eyes smouldered as he glimpsed the mixture of conflicting emotions chasing across her expressive features. With a husky laugh he pulled her close and strode purposefully from the lounge towards the stairs leading to their elegantly-appointed bedroom at the far end of the hallway.

With an adroit movement he closed the door behind them, then moving towards the bed he gently lowered her to stand at its edge.

'What about dinner?' she murmured, and his answering smile did strange things to her equilibrium.

'Who cares about food?'

She stood transfixed by the deep slumbrous ardency of his gaze, and there wasn't a thing she could do to stop him as he slowly divested her of every last vestige of clothing.

'Undress me,' Rafael instructed, and when she didn't comply he caught hold of her hands and placed them against his broad chest. 'Don't be shy, *querida.*' His lips descended to each eyelid in turn, then trailed the slope of her nose before seeking the sensitive hollows at the base of her throat. Each pulsebeat was the recipient of that warm probing mouth as it traversed the gentle swell of her breasts to tease first one tautened rosy peak before crossing to render a similar treatment to the other.

Just when she thought she could stand no more his hands began a slow feathery path over her supple young body, his touch akin to a virtuoso as he played each sensitive nerve to its ultimate sensual pitch, so that she became an enchanted wild thing, ready and willing to do anything he asked of her.

As if in a dream she reached for the buttons on his shirt, and when they were undone she pulled it from him, easing it off his powerful shoulders and letting it fall to the carpet as her fingers sought the buckle at the waist of his trousers.

'Touch me, *querida*, as I touch you,' he directed softly, smiling a little as she hesitated. 'Don't be ashamed. Making love is more than just the joining of two bodies in sexual copulation. It is the mutual giving of pleasure, heightening the senses to a degree beyond mindless passion.'

Sara wanted to cry from the sheer physical bliss he was able to create as his mouth and hands took hitherto unexplored liberties until she arched against him like a wanton craving fulfilment.

'Rafael, please! I can't stand any more,' she moaned, uncaring that she begged a merciful release.

He didn't comply at once, and her breath rasped

in her throat as she unashamedly sobbed his name, frustrated tears spilling from her eyes to run unnoticed down her cheeks until with a husky growl he covered her body with his own.

The wild creature that rose and twisted beneath him to meet and surpass his passion confounded and dismayed her in the aftermath as she lay in his encircling arms.

Drowsiness was soon replaced by sleep, and even in its unconscious state her body curved into his, almost as if they were twin halves of a whole.

CHAPTER NINE

IT was late when Sara woke next morning, and she moved cautiously, stretching with the supine laziness of a cat who has been satiated to the fullest extent. Slowly she turned her head and saw that she was alone in the middle of that great bed, and she twisted round to glimpse the time from the bedside clock.

It couldn't be *ten*, surely? She raised herself on an elbow and leaned closer, her eyes widening with disbelief as she was presented with the proof. With a groan she rolled on to her stomach and buried her head beneath the pillow.

Like a kaleidoscope, events from the previous night appeared before her in a wild complexity of sequence, and with a gesture of impotence she curled her fists into a ball and beat them against the unprotesting mattress.

How could she have submitted to such decadent lasciviousness? It didn't bear thinking about.

One thing was certain, she couldn't lie in bed all morning commiserating her fate. *Bed*—the instrument of her downfall. Oh, how she wished she'd never been born!

Then she sobered, shivering slightly in the knowledge that if that were so, she would never have experienced the heights of sensual awareness in the arms of a man she had come to love. *Love?* Was that the emotion responsible for the way she felt? A deep pulsing ache that gnawed at her subconscious until she could think of little else? Love was supposed to be a warm merging of two spirits, an affection that brought two people together on a plateau far above the bonds of friendship. The wild physical passion she shared with Rafael could only be lust, which when slaked left her hating him with all of her former fervour.

Sara gave a groan of despair. Whenever he was within sight she couldn't even *think*. How was she ever going to get anything into its proper perspective seeing him every day, every *night*?

With sudden clarity she knew there could be only one remedy. She had to get away, somewhere where she could be alone and free from his disturbing presence.

The question was—*where*? Not with Selina. That would be the first place he would look. Not the penthouse suite either, for undoubtedly that would come under search as well. It had to be a nondescript motel, somewhere remote in likelihood, if not in distance.

Sliding out from between the sheets, Sara made for the bathroom, emerging several minutes later to dress, then, satisfied with her appearance, she extracted a suitcase and chose clothes at random, sufficient for three or four days.

Her main concern was leaving the house undetected, but neither Tomás nor Clara were in evidence as she descended the stairs and slipped out the door. Now she had only to put her suitcase into the boot of whichever car Rafael had left in the garage. A slight grimace pursed her lips. She hoped he'd taken the Lamborghini, for she was loath to take the wheel of that powerful machine, or if it came to that, the Mercedes.

Luck was in her favour, for the Porsche rested in its usual place in the large garage, and without undue haste she deposited her suitcase, then slid into the driver's seat and reversed out on to the wide sweeping driveway. Minutes later she was motoring towards the main highway south.

Unsure of her destination, she simply drove, her only concern being to put as many miles between herself and her formidable husband as possible. Later she would have time to reflect on such a rash decision, but now she put it firmly out of her head.

The consequences of her actions weren't something she wanted to dwell on, for instinct warned that Rafael would be a dangerous man to cross, and his anger would doubtless bring retribution upon her head.

Dear God, she hadn't left so much as a note telling him of her intention. If he contacted Selina as to her whereabouts, her mother would become anxious, and that was something to be avoided at any cost.

Tugan, Bilinga, Coolangatta—she drove through each without noticing, slowing slightly in obedience of the imposed speed limit, then letting the needle ease up again without conscious awareness.

From Tweed Heads she drove via Murwillumba and Byron Bay to Ballina where she turned in to the first motel on the outskirts of town. After booking in, she followed the manageress to a small cheerfully decorated unit, and as soon as she was alone she caught up the phone and dialled the boutique.

'Selina? Have you a few minutes in which to talk, or are you busy?'

'One customer, darling, but she's only browsing. What is it, Sara?'

'I've decided to have a few days on my own,' Sara began without preamble. 'Rafael doesn't know—I forgot to leave him a note.'

'That's very remiss of you,' her mother chided. 'You'd better ring him at once. He'll be concerned.'

Would he? She doubted it! Angry that she'd had the temerity to go against him—but concern? Only people who cared became concerned over another's actions.

'It may be difficult for me to contact him,' she declared matter-of-factly. 'Would you mind assuring him that I'm okay?'

'Sara, this isn't at all like you. What's the matter? Have you and Rafael quarrelled?'

Oh lord, what could she say? 'Nothing like that,' she said quickly. 'Look, don't worry—I'll ring him myself. I just thought I should warn you that he may contact you, and I didn't want you to worry. I'm perfectly fine—really.'

'You don't sound it, darling. Hadn't you better tell me where you are?'

'There's no point, I may be moving on in a few hours.' This was getting more difficult by the minute. 'Look, I have to go. I'll ring you again tomorrow.' Sara replaced the receiver slowly, then turned to gaze sightlessly round the room.

It was late afternoon, and her rumbling stomach reminded her that she hadn't eaten all day. She felt lightheaded and rather strange. If she was going to gather sufficient strength to contact Rafael, then it would be better to do it on a full stomach!

She crossed to the small kitchenette and checked cupboards and the refrigerator, seeing at a glance there was little more than sachets of coffee, sugar and milk powder. Damn! A motel this size probably wouldn't run to an adjoining restaurant, and she hadn't thought to stop on the way to pick up any provisions.

There was only one answer, and suiting thought to action she collected up her purse and keys and went out to the car. Takeaways didn't hold much appeal, and it was almost half an hour before she returned, complete with her assorted purchases.

At six o'clock she sat down to an appetising meal of grilled steak, fried mushrooms, and freshly tossed salad. There was a crisp bread roll to go with it, and followed by strong black sugared coffee it did much to restore her libido.

Now she felt ready to tackle Rafael, although she didn't exactly relish the task. Tomás answered, and she had barely identified herself when Rafael came on the line.

'Sara? Where in the name of heaven are you?' His voice was deep with suppressed fury, and she winced and held the receiver away from her ear.

'Enjoying a well-earned break,' she answered with succinct sarcasm. 'I have every intention of returning before Ana gets back from her school camp at the end of the week, so there's no cause for alarm.'

Rafael's answering oath was muffled, and she could sense his anger emanating down the line. 'Sara,' he warned dangerously, 'come home at once—do you understand?'

'No.' Dear God, how could she sound so calm? 'I'm quite capable of taking care of myself for a few days.'

'Where are you?' he demanded emotively

'Oh no, Rafael,' she refused with a hollow laugh. 'If I tell you that, you'll appear and drag me back.' A lump caught in her throat and it took a few seconds for her to continue. 'The whole idea is for me to get away from you.'

'What do you hope to achieve, for God's sake?'

'You—stifle me,' she answered shakily. 'I'll be back on Friday—I promise.'

His silence frightened her, and she quickly replaced the receiver, almost as if by holding on to it she gave him the power to determine her whereabouts.

The simple chore of clearing the few dishes she'd used didn't succeed in wiping out his compelling image, and in desperation she crossed to the television set and switched it on in the hope that one of the many channels might provide some light entertainment.

Figures danced across the screen with colourful movement, and she forced herself to view a comedy show before changing to a documentary, which in normal circumstances would have held her undivided attention.

Damn, damn, *damn*! What was the matter with her? She felt sick, sickened, and totally disorientated. All she could think of was Rafael. The way his dark hair curled back from a powerful forehead. Eyes as dark as ebony in a face whose rugged lines were intensely masculine. His mouth, whose sensual lips could tease and tantalise, or alternatively bruise with cruel intent. She knew every nuance in that faintly-accented voice, could sense his mood as if it was an extension of her own.

Oh hell, she cursed with utter dejection. Maybe if she went to bed, sleep would provide a blissful oblivion. A glance at her watch revealed that it was only nine o'clock, but the long drive had tired her, and with a sigh she rose to her feet and made for the bathroom.

After a leisurely shower she donned her nightgown and slid in between the sheets of the comfortable-looking bed, then she raised her hand and extinguished the bedlamp.

The night was long and lonely, and although Sara knew she must have slipped into a fitful doze from time to time, she rose in the morning hardly aware of having slept at all.

One thing emerged clearly from those wakeful hours: she loved Rafael. Only love could be responsible for this endless aching need that was almost an obsession. He was the other half of her, and she knew that without him she might as well not be alive.

The decision to go back was made without conscious thought, and after a hasty cup of coffee and a slice of toast Sara slid her nightgown into her overnight bag and deposited it in the car.

She was on the road by nine, and as she covered the miles her heart seemed to soar and take flight. Already she was planning how she would surprise him. Without any unforeseen delay she should reach Southport by midday, and a light smile curved her lips as she imagined his reaction when she walked into his office and invited him to take her to lunch.

Just past Murwillumba there was a build-up of traffic and Sara slowed the Porsche to slip in behind the car ahead.

What happened next remained a blur. She felt and heard simultaneously a sickening thud, and she was flung forward before she could steel herself to prevent it, then there was nothing.

Vaguely in the distance she could hear the wail of sirens, and through the mists of unconsciousness she was aware of voices, hands that freed and lifted her, a sensation of pain, and a delicious floating feeling.

When at last she regained consciousness it was to see an unknown face smiling down on her, and as her eyes slowly adjusted she saw the neat white uniform and heard the pleasant voice say briskly,

'You've decided to wake at last. How do you feel?'

'I'm still floating,' Sara found herself saying, discovering that she felt very delicate indeed. 'Am I hurt? I don't feel as if I am, yet I don't think I could get out of bed.'

'Doctor will be in to see you in a minute. He'll discuss the extent of your injuries with you then. In the meantime, I'll give you an injection which will make you feel rather drowsy. Just press this button if you need me,' the nurse said kindly, reaching out and placing an electric buzzer on the bed beside Sara's hand.

The doctor was far more forthright. 'A bump on the head which will probably ache abominably over the next few days. Aside from that, a few lacerations and a cracked rib. You're a very lucky young woman, Mrs Savalje. It could have been a lot worse.'

'You know my name?' Her eyes flew wide, and he smiled.

'Your husband has been here for the past few hours. He's waiting outside to see you.'

Rafael—here? Her face paled slightly, and his eyes narrowed in thoughtful speculation.

'Do you want me to tell him to return in the morning?'

Sara moved her head in negation, then winced as pain shot ingloriously from her forehead through to the base of her skull. 'No, of course not.'

With a slight nod the young doctor turned on his heel and strode quickly from the room, and in a moment of blind panic Sara closed her eyes in the hope that all this was a bad dream.

'Hello, Sara.'

That deep drawl was achingly familiar, and *real*. Her eyelids slowly flickered open, and she regarded him with unblinking solemnity, acknowledging cautiously, 'Rafael.'

There was nothing she could tell from his enigmatic expression, and her eyes widened slightly as he moved towards her from the lower end of the bed. In the need to say something—anything, she let the words pour out in a breathless rush. 'The Porsche—I hope it isn't too badly damaged. It——' Her words were effectively silenced as his mouth closed over hers.

'Shut up, you little fool,' he muttered huskily seconds later. 'I don't give a damn about the car.'

Her ribs hurt as her breathing quickened, and her eyes widened immeasurably as he sat down on the edge of the bed beside her.

'It wasn't my fault,' she offered shakily, becoming caught up in the spell of him.

'Oh, Sara,' Rafael shook his head wryly. 'What am I to do with you?'

A convulsive gulp momentarily choked her. 'You'd have done better not to have married me.'

Without a word he reached out and trailed his fingers gently down her cheek. 'You think so?'

To her utter consternation she felt her eyes filling with tears. 'Oh damn,' she cursed shakily.

'Don't cry, *querida*,' he chided softly. 'Otherwise the good nurses will imagine you find my visit upsetting, and I'll be asked to leave.'

'Perhaps you'd better, anyway,' Sara said wretchedly. 'I don't feel myself at all.'

'You've been wandering in and out of consciousness for several hours,' Rafael revealed with a strangely taut smile, and he rose to his feet to tower over her. 'Rest easy, *pequeña*.' His eyes darkened with an indefinable emotion. 'I'll be here if you need me.' He leaned down and brushed her cheek with his lips, then straightening he turned and walked to the door.

Things were hazy after that as she drifted in and out of sleep, waking once during the evening to sip a cooling drink before slipping once again into a deep dreamless sleep. At some stage of the night or early morning she woke in darkness, sure that she had cried out. The soft pad of feet and the rustle of a uniform testified that she had, and she felt the prick of a needle and heard a few soothing words before everything became obscured in a dark grey void.

Sara woke in the morning to the sound of breakfast trolleys and the general bustle of hospital activity. Sun streamed in through partially shuttered louvre blinds, and she slid up to sit leaning against her pillows, conscious that although her head still ached, the woolliness that had been evident was now mercifully gone.

The door swung open and a figure swept in and adjusted the blinds. 'Ah, you are awake. How do you feel?'

'Better,' Sara smiled gingerly, extending her wrist to have her pulse taken.

'Hm, yes, I think you are,' the nurse declared with customary briskness. 'Doctor will be in shortly.' She shook down a thermometer and slipped it beneath Sara's tongue. 'Headache less painful?'

Sara gave a slight indicative nod, and moments later the nurse took the glass tube from her mouth to record its reading on to a chart.

'There'll be a cup of tea for you in a minute.' With a brief smile the nurse turned and left.

Mid-morning brought the arrival of flowers—huge bunched arrangements in a glorious assortment of colours, and as the cellophane was unwrapped from each and vases found, Sara became something of a personage among the nurses. She read the accompanying cards; two were from Selina, one from Silvia, and the rest bore Rafael's bold signature.

Afternoon visiting hours heralded the arrival of Selina accompanied by Rafael, and Sara eyed the small package he dropped on to her lap with mixed pleasure.

'What is it?'

His smile was totally without mockery, and she felt her eyes widen at the lambent warmth evident in those dark eyes as they regarded her with quizzical amusement. 'Open it and see for yourself.'

Her fingers were faintly shaky as they undid the wrapping, and she sprang open the flat jeweller's box to reveal an obviously expensive gold medallion on a fine gold chain. 'St Christopher!' Her exclamation brought an answering chuckle.

'Wear it, *querida*,' he directed gently, moving forward to extract it from its box, and unclasping the fastening he brushed aside her hair and placed it round her neck.

Sara felt a tingle where his fingers touched against her skin, and his close proximity made breathing difficult. The clean male smell of him plus an elusive tang of aftershave was intoxicating, and in that moment she longed to feel his mouth on hers.

At that precise moment his eyes caught hers, and her lips parted in wistful expectation as she murmured her thanks. Then without thought she raised her hands and slipped them round his neck, pulling his head down so she could kiss him.

It was a shy tentative gesture, and as she drew back there was a quizzical gleam in the depths of his dark eyes.

On a long chain the medallion rested in the valley between her breasts, and she glanced at it before raising her eyes to meet his. 'It's beautiful.'

'I agree.' Rafael was looking at her, his meaning unmistakable, and there was no way she could hide the faint blush that rose to her cheeks.

'Thank you for the flowers,' Sara said quietly, moving her gaze to include Selina. 'They're lovely.' A slight smile curved her lips. 'I'm being spoilt.'

'You gave us all a nasty fright,' Selina told her, and she suppressed a shudder. 'Rafael summoned specialists from as far away as Sydney, and he never left the hospital until this morning.'

'Specialists? But all I had was a cracked rib and a bruise on my head,' she said incredulously, then doubt clouded her features as she queried, 'This is the main public hospital, isn't it?'

'I'm afraid not,' her mother said gently. 'Rafael insisted you receive the best possible medical attention.'

'I see,' Sara said faintly. 'When am I allowed to go home?'

'In a few days,' Rafael told her. 'We'll leave it up to the good doctor to decide.'

Those few days seemed to pass very slowly, despite the fact Sara had visitors both afternoon and evening. Even more flowers arrived, and her room began to look like an exotic glasshouse, so that one nurse was known to say jokingly that they had to look hard to find her among them all.

Rafael called in more than once each day, and was always there during the evening. His presence caused more than a flutter among the nurses, and his dedicated attendance was the subject of many sighs and wistful glances.

Ana was permitted to visit on Friday evening, having returned that afternoon from a week at summer camp, and her eyes were almost as round as saucers as she came into the room.

'Oh, Sara,' she breathed in a voice little above a whisper, 'are you really all right?'

Sara felt her heart turn over at the concern in the little girl's voice, and she smiled and held out her hand. 'Really,' she assured her. 'I can't be squeezed for a while, that's all.'

Ana moved forward and her mouth began to quiver as she looked at the exposed wound on Sara's forehead. 'Does it hurt?'

'Not now,' Sara said gently. 'It's turning all colours of the rainbow, and I may have to buy some eyeshadow to match it,' she finished with a smile.

'It was just as well you were wearing your safety-belt,' the little girl declared gravely. 'When are you coming home?'

'Tomorrow,' Rafael told her laconically, and he leant over to bestow a light kiss to Sara's cheek.

'Papa, why didn't you tell me?' Ana clapped her hands and a huge smile lit her features. 'Clara and Tomás will be pleased. So will Grandmama.'

'We'll all be relieved to have Sara home where she belongs,' he said quietly, and Sara had to glance away from his dark penetrating gaze.

'Tell me about your school trip,' she invited Ana, who at once related every exciting detail with the enthusiasm of the very young.

'I have lots of samples and notes,' Ana finished. 'I'll show them to you tomorrow.'

'I'll look forward to it,' Sara said solemnly.

'Well, *pequeña*, we shall get away, hm?' Rafael directed, and reaching out a hand he ruffled her shiny black hair. 'It won't do to overtire Sara.'

His kiss was brief, yet gentle, and left Sara feeling strangely bereft. For the first time since the accident she slept badly, and in the morning she woke feeling as if she hadn't slept at all.

When Rafael arrived at ten, Sara was dressed and waiting for him. The doctor had already been and formally discharged her, giving her a prescription in case the headaches should recur, and had added the admonition that if they were at all severe or lasted more than a few hours she must get in touch with him at once.

'Are you ready?'

Sara stood to her feet and proffered a slight smile. 'Yes. You didn't bring Ana with you?'

Rafael bent down and caught up her suitcase. 'I thought it best if she waited at home.'

In the car Sara was quiet—subdued was a better word for it, she thought wryly. More than once she began to say something, then halted before the words found voice, sure that it would sound inane and contrived. However, the silence was enervating, and in a fit of desperation she said, 'How's the Porsche—is the damage severe?'

'That's the least of my worries, Sara,' Rafael drawled lazily, taking his eyes from the road momentarily to shoot her a penetrating glance.

'You've been very kind these past few days,' she told him carefully. 'Thank you.'

'What did you expect, *querida*?' he slanted sardonically. 'A tyrannical raging bull?'

She was helpless in controlling the smile that rose to her lips. 'You have been exactly that on occasion.'

'While you, of course, have been an example of docility, eh?'

'We come from different backgrounds, Rafael,' Sara said with a degree of sadness. 'And if I lived for another hundred years, I could never match your particular brand of sophistication. Sometimes I think you were born having lived another life to the utmost extent.'

'And that bothers you?'

'Only that I must seem gauche and naïve by comparison.'

'Oh, Sara,' he mocked gently, 'you are in a state of confusion, aren't you?'

Suddenly brave, she ventured, 'That's why I went away.'

'It was the method you employed I can't be expected to condone.'

'You were angry,' she stated unnecessarily, and glimpsed his grim smile.

'Really, *querida*, did you expect me not to be?'

'No, I suppose not,' Sara agreed in a small voice, and very close to tears, she turned and gazed out the window, trying valiantly to take interest in the swiftly passing scenery.

'*Dios!*' The angry oath escaped his lips in a husky growl. 'Your timing is bad, Sara,' he bit out emotively. 'In the midst of traffic on the main highway you want an emotional blow-by-blow account of my feelings in the matter?'

'I'm sorry,' she whispered disconsolately, and winced against his string of Spanish epithets.

'We need to talk,' he declared with great restraint. 'But this is neither the time nor the place.'

'I'm sorry,' Sara repeated, and flinched at the look he threw in her direction.

'Dear God, if you so much as apologise once more, I swear I won't be held responsible for my actions!'

Silence was obviously the safest course, and Sara refrained from uttering so much as another word for what remained of the drive home.

CHAPTER TEN

SARA's arrival at the elegant mansion was greeted with unsolicited enthusiasm from Ana and Silvia, both of whom had obviously been hovering at a nearby window, from the speed in which the front door opened the instant the Lamborghini drew to a halt at the head of the sweeping drive-way.

Amidst laughter and a few tears Sara was ushered inside, and, safely ensconced on a comfortable chair in the lounge, she gave every appearance of being relaxed as Clara wheeled in a portable trolley on which reposed a delicious array of cakes and savour-ies, together with a pot containing hot steaming coffee.

Thanks to Silvia and Ana there was little op-portunity for a lull in conversation, and when the leisurely morning tea was over Rafael regretfully took his leave, bidding Sara a stern admonition to rest and not over-exert herself. His parting kiss had just the right degree of warmth, but Sara was all too aware that the gesture was solely for Silvia and Ana's benefit.

The day passed with amazing rapidity, and as the hour approached for Rafael's return Sara became increasingly tense and on edge, so that his arrival was almost a relief.

Dinner was a convivial meal comprising three courses and accompanied by an excellent wine. To any onlooker they presented an enviable tableau, and if Silvia was aware of any undercurrent between her son and daughter-in-law she gave no sign, and Ana, bless her, seemed oblivious to all in her delight at having Sara home.

At eight o'clock Rafael brooked little argument from Ana over her bedtime, and scarcely an hour later he intimated that Sara should retire.

'You look all eyes, *querida*,' he admonished gently. 'Come, I will see you upstairs, hm?'

Sara shot him a look that quelled beneath the guise of a smile. 'There's no need. I doubt I'll collapse on the stairs.'

'Humour me, *niña*,' he drawled, coming to stand beside her chair, and the smile he slanted her held a hint of warning.

Without a word she rose to her feet, and after bidding Silvia an affectionate goodnight, she preceded Rafael from the room, crossing the wide entrance hall and mounting the stairs ahead of him.

'I'm not a child,' she said crossly as soon as the bedroom door had closed behind them.

'Did I imply that you were?' He moved slowly towards her to halt less than a foot away, and she eyed him warily, unsure of his intention.

'You don't need to tuck me into bed. I can manage quite well on my own.' If he touched her, she'd be lost, and that would never do.

'Nevertheless, I will see you safely between the sheets.'

'Rafael——'

'I insist,' he told her silkily, and she turned away defeated.

'I'd like a shower.' She moved towards the adjoining bathroom, uncaring whether he followed or not. Despite her argument to the contrary she was tired, and the thought of slipping between cool clean sheets was more welcoming than she was willing to admit.

The warm needlespray proved relaxing, and she emerged from the glass cubicle to find Rafael's tall frame leaning with indolent ease against the doorjamb. Without a word she reached for a towel and wrapped it sarong-wise about her slim form.

He moved then, untucking the edge of the towel from between her breasts, and with infinite care he began to dry the moisture from her body.

There were bruises in various hues over much of her ribcage, and his lips tightened at the sight of them peeping above and below the adhesive bandage.

'It looks much worse than it is,' Sara discounted, torn between a desire to laugh and cry.

'You're fortunate to be alive,' Rafael told her with unnecessary harshness, and she stepped backwards in an endeavour to move away from him.

'There are times when I wish I weren't,' she flung wretchedly, and his eyes hardened into ebony chips.

'Don't be childish.'

'Oh, leave me alone!' Sara cried, and her eyes were wide with pain as she looked at him. 'I don't need your ministrations.' To her chagrin she felt her lower lip tremble. 'Can't I have any privacy at all?'

For a moment his expression was incredibly bleak, then he handed her the towel and turned on his heel. 'I'll wait in the bedroom.'

Warm tears slid ignominiously down her cheeks, and it took all her strength to complete her toilette before returning to face him.

'You have some tablets to take.' His dark eyes swept her slim nightgown-clad frame, and without a word she crossed to take the tablets and glass of water from his outstretched hand, swallowing them with ease, then she moved to the large bed and slid in between the covers.

'You're quite comfortable?'

No, she wanted to scream. I have a giant-size ache around the region of my heart, and it's all due to *you*. 'Thank you.' Oh God, how polite she sounded! She closed her eyes against the sight of him, and heard the faint click as he switched off the light, then the sound of the bedroom door closing as he departed.

It was then that the tears came. Soundless and soft, they rolled slowly down her cheeks to slip off the edge of her chin.

In the days that followed there was little change in the pattern of Sara's existence. She rose late after breakfasting in bed, then after a shower she descended downstairs to spend what was left of the morning wandering aimlessly in Clara's wake before taking a leisurely lunch with Silvia. Ana's arrival home from school became the highlight of her life as she supervised homework and queried the happenings in the little girl's day. Her retirement upstairs to change for dinner was inevitably timed to coincide with Rafael's arrival home, and by careful planning she ensured her entrance into the lounge came within minutes to that of Silvia.

It was the night hours that were the worst, for then Sara would lie in bed sleepless, waiting with a heavy heart for Rafael to come upstairs, hopeful yet partly afraid that he might choose that night to take her in his arms. Yet without exception he entered the bedroom long after she had slipped beneath the sheets, and after a leisurely shower he would slide in beside her to lie within touching distance. Before long his deep breathing indicated that he had fallen asleep, and never had she felt more like hitting him.

Precisely one week after Sara's arrival home from hospital Silvia took Rafael to task over dinner.

'Why not take Sara out for a few hours?' she suggested tentatively, meeting her son's dark gaze with fearless ease. 'It would do her good.'

'Yes, Papa,' Ana endorsed with an eagerness Sara could only applaud. 'It must be dull for her sitting around the house all day. She's much better,' the little girl added, turning to enquire earnestly, 'Aren't you, Sara?'

'Much,' she responded quickly, not quite meeting his gaze.

'I think this is a conspiracy,' Rafael drawled lazily. 'In the face of three determined females, what chance does a mere male have but to conform gracefully?' He directed Sara a penetrating glance. '*Do* you feel up to a few hours' socialising?'

'Yes,' she answered with alacrity, and he chuckled.

'All right, *querida*, so be it. Go and repair your make-up, and we'll be on our way.'

'Now?' Sara queried, astounded at his acquiescence.

'I don't intend allowing you to overdo things by staying out until all hours of the night.'

She gave a slight grimace, tempering it with a smile for Silvia and Ana's benefit. 'Like Cinderella, I'm to be delivered home by midnight.'

His lips twisted with faint mockery. 'A pity I'm not the magic prince.'

'The prince managed to find Cinderella in the

end,' Ana declared with childish insouciance, and Rafael laughed.

'Indeed he did, *niña*.'

Ten minutes later Sara was seated in the Lamborghini as Rafael headed it towards Surfer's Paradise.

'Is there anywhere in particular you'd like to go?'

She considered the question carefully. 'Somewhere quiet and not too noisy. I'll leave it to you.'

His choice turned out to be an exclusive nightclub on the edge of town, and it was a purely nervous gesture that prompted her to finger the almost indistinguishable bruise on her forehead.

'It doesn't show, Sara,' he assured her quietly as they neared the main entrance. 'Say when you're tired, and we'll go home.'

The maître d'hotel found them a corner table, and Rafael ordered champagne, 'In honour of your return to health,' he explained with a slight smile as she questioned his choice.

'You're being very—solicitous,' she said politely, and his eyes gleamed with quizzical amusement.

'Are you suggesting I have been remiss in some way?'

'Of course not,' she managed evenly, trying to ignore the way her pulse began to quicken as he regarded her.

'I have to make a business trip to Sydney next week,' he said slowly, and her eyelids flickered impassively.

'Oh?' She tried to sound unconcerned, and failed dismally. 'How long will you be away?'

'A week—maybe longer.'

'I see.'

His lips twisted into a faint smile. 'You sound almost regretful. Are you?'

'Should I be?' Sara countered lightly.

'It's not unknown for wives to accompany their husbands on business.'

'Is that a statement or an invitation?'

Mockery lit his eyes. 'Would you come if I asked?'

'If that's what you want,' she responded evenly, and he uttered a wry laugh.

'Since when have you taken my feelings into consideration, Sara?'

His taunting cynicism touched a raw nerve. 'I know what you want, Rafael. What I haven't figured out is why.'

'Oh, it's quite simple,' he mocked gently. 'Even Ana could supply the answer.'

'In that case, I shouldn't find it too difficult.'

'It's right beneath your nose, *querida*, yet you fail to recognise it.'

'Rafael!'

They both turned at the sound of a feminine voice husky with deliberate seductiveness, and Sara felt a shaft of pain stab her heart as she saw Renée glide sinuously towards their table.

'Renée.' Rafael stood to his feet in a formal gesture, the polite smile on his lips nowhere near reaching his eyes.

'Darling, I was hoping to find you here tonight,' Renée declared breathlessly, reaching out to touch his arm in a clinging possessive gesture, and the way she was looking at him was positively sickening.

'Indeed?'

The stunning redhead darted a quick glance towards Sara, dismissed her in an instant, then she swung back to Rafael with a coaxing smile. 'Aren't you going to ask me to join you?'

'But of course.' His response was smooth, but Sara

sensed the anger beneath the surface and was idly fascinated.

Renée took the chair he held out, and when he was seated he bade the hovering waiter bring another glass.

'Champers, darling? Are you celebrating or something?'

'Merely the pleasure in bringing my wife out for the evening,' he replied with every indication of geniality, and Renée was forced to acknowledge Sara's presence.

'Oh yes—you smashed up the Porsche.'

So much for compassionate solicitude, Sara thought wryly, and with a sweet smile she answered, 'Thank you, I'm fine now.'

'You should have been more careful.'

Sara started to open her mouth, then closed it again, and reached for her glass.

'Did you come alone?'

At Rafael's query the other woman laughed, and with a slight shrugging gesture she made a pouting moue. 'Basil is busy parking the car, I imagine.'

'He has just come in,' Rafael intimated as his sweeping gaze caught the elegantly-suited man engaged in conversation at the front desk. He signalled, and the next instant Renée's companion of the evening was moving to join them.

Another bottle of champagne joined the almost empty one on the table as the waiter refilled their glasses.

'Shall I propose a toast?' Rafael indicated with urbane equanimity, and Renée uttered a delighted laugh.

'Of course, darling. Go ahead.'

'To the moment of truth,' he mocked lightly, raising his glass and touching it against that of Sara's before lifting it to his lips.

'Good heavens!' Renée tinkled with a faint air of perplexity. 'Is this some private joke, or may we all share in it?'

'I want you to apologise to Sara for fabricating a tissue of lies about your supposed relationship with me.'

Dear lord! He had the timing of a deadly cobra! Sara sat mesmerised as if she herself were caught beneath that hypnotic reptilian spell, totally fascinated with her husband's cool implacability.

'Really, Rafael, I have no idea what you're talking about.'

'I beg to differ.' His eyes never left hers, and Sara suppressed a shiver at the pitiless disregard evident in those unfathomable depths.

'Rafael,' Renée pouted prettily, 'this is hardly the time or place to discuss such——' she paused delicately—'intimacies.'

'There haven't been any "intimacies", as you call it,' he drawled, 'for several years. Is that not so?'

The other woman's eyes glittered with bitter enmity. 'Your taste is deplorable, darling. You'd have done better to have employed her as a nanny. Her qualifications are infinitely more suited to supervising a child, than satisfying a virile sensual male.' Her voice rose a fraction in vindictive vilification. 'Is she a receptive pupil, Rafael? I'm inclined to pity you if she's not.' She lifted her glass and tossed back the contents in one elegant swallow, then swung round to her silent companion. 'Let's go on somewhere else, sweetie. This place has suddenly lost its appeal.' She stood to her feet in one fluid movement, then she swept away from the table without so much as a backward glance.

'I'm—er—sorry,' Basil began awkwardly, rising to his feet and giving every indication of being totally embarrassed by the recent scene. 'Renée is——' he foundered helplessly, and Rafael interjected silkily,

'Don't apologise.'

'Unfortunate,' Basil murmured, going slightly pink around the ears, and Sara couldn't help but feel sorry for him. He was way out of his depth and knew it.

'Goodnight,' Rafael drawled significantly, and with a strangled rejoinder the other man fled.

Sara drew a deep steadying breath and reached for her glass, sipping a generous quantity before replacing it down on to the table. 'You were perfectly horrid,' she said slowly, and his expression assumed musing cynicism.

'It had the desired effect.'

She met his gaze with difficulty. 'Did you know she was going to be here tonight?'

'Renée is familiar with most of my usual haunts,' Rafael intimated dryly.

'I see.'

His lips twisted into a slight smile. 'What do you see, *querida*?'

'You're quite ruthless, aren't you?' she countered, and saw his eyes darken.

'I protect my own.'

'Like a lion at bay,' Sara remarked wryly, and heard his husky chuckle.

'Would you rather I had not defended you?'

She swallowed convulsively and held his quizzical gaze. 'No. Thank you,' she added politely.

'Oh, Sara, what a confounding little baggage you are,' he mocked gently, and reaching out an idle hand he pushed a stray lock of hair back behind her ear. 'There are times when I despair I have *two* children on my hands.' His fingers moved down to tilt her chin. 'Come, *querida*, let's go home, hm? I think you have had enough for one night.'

Where was all her former fire? Like a docile lamb she rose from the table and followed him out to the car, to sit in contemplative silence all the way home.

'You're very quiet.'

Sara glanced across the room as he snapped the door shut, and her heart began a series of painful somersaults. He looked totally at ease, yet there was a leashed quality about him that hinted—what? Anger, passion? She couldn't tell. 'It's been quite a day,' she offered, and crossing to the bed she extracted the silky slither of fabric that was her nightgown. She felt dejected and completely enervated, yet attuned to the fine element of danger that seemed to reverberate around the room. More than anything she wanted to say, 'Hold me. Love me, as I love you'. But the words seemed to stick in her throat, and with a gesture of impotence she turned towards the bathroom, only to come to an abrupt halt as hard hands steadied her flight.

Her eyes swept up to meet Rafael's and she almost cried as she glimpsed the surge of emotion evident in those dark depths. 'I—owe you an apology,' she began shakily. Nothing mattered any more, for she had no pride left where he was concerned. 'I love you.' The words left her lips as an inaudible whisper he had to bend low to catch, and she felt rather than heard the breath expel slowly from his body in an emotive drawn-out sigh.

Gently his lips brushed her forehead, caressing the slight tenderness where the bruise had been, then he lifted his head to regard her with such naked desire she was powerless to stop the blush that rose to her cheeks.

'You apologise for loving me?' he demanded gently, and his hands lifted to circle her throat, tilting her chin so she had to look at him.

'For doubting you.'

'Renée can be convincing.'

She managed a tentative shaky smile. 'Very.' Her tongue edged along her lower lip in a nervous gesture. 'She took pleasure in paying me the doubtful compliment of not rearranging the furniture in your penthouse apartment.'

His expression tautened into a hard implacable mask. 'It was a regrettable lapse on the part of one of my employees that she managed to inveigle an appointment to view the apartment.' At her apparent puzzlement, he gave a faint smile. 'I have decided to lease it,' he explained, his expression softening as he added gently, 'I no longer have need of the privacy it affords.'

Comprehension brought a blush to her cheeks, and her lips parted soundlessly. 'Oh,' she breathed quietly. 'That explains how she came to be there.'

'I will never forgive her for being instrumental in driving you away.' Dark eyes smouldered down at her, leaving her wide-eyed and trembling at the latent wrath beneath the surface. 'Nor for the fact that you were in the wrong place at the wrong time and suffered injury.' He paled in painful reflection. '*Dios*, you could have been killed!'

Sara placed her fingers over his mouth in a conciliatory gesture, and felt his lips part beneath that butterfly touch. 'I was on my way back,' she began quietly, conscious of the way her pulse began to race as he caught her hand and kissed each finger in turn.

'I discovered I loved you—so much, that it didn't matter if you didn't love me in return.' Her lower lip trembled slightly, and she met his gaze fearlessly. 'It was enough that I was your wife.'

Rafael began to speak, only she shook her head. 'Please—let me finish.' A laugh choked in her throat. 'I may never have the courage again. I tried to tell you after the accident,' she continued tremulously. 'If you had taken me in your arms, just once, I don't think I could have helped myself. But you didn't,' she finished forlornly, then he was kissing her with such gentle hunger she thought she would die from it.

'Sara,' he groaned huskily. 'Have you any conception what I went through at the hospital? Endless hours of waiting for you to regain consciousness, not knowing the full extent of your injuries, and feeling so damned *helpless*.' He gave an emotive growl, and for a brief second his expression became harsh and forbidding. 'Didn't you look in a mirror—not *once* during the past few weeks? How could I trust myself to touch you? My God, every time I came near you, all I could see was that massive bruise covering part of your pale fragile face. And your ribs,' he added brusquely, sparing her a wry glance. 'Can you imagine how much pain I could have inflicted had I forgotten in a moment of passion? No, *querida*, it was far better to leave you alone.'

'I thought you didn't want me any more,' she voiced slowly, and caught his quizzical gleam.

'If you knew how many cold showers I've taken over the past few days you wouldn't say that!'

Her lips curved into a singularly winsome smile. 'I think I can safely guarantee you've seen the last of those.'

'Mm, is that an invitation?'

'You bet your sweet life!' Sara told him with bewitching candour, and he laughed, his dark eyes agleam with devilish humour as he drew her close.

'Well, in that case, I guess I'd better do something about it.' His mouth descended to cover hers, and he kissed her with such piercing sweetness it was all she could do not to cry. 'Tears, *querida*?' he husked gently as he tasted the first salty rivulet that fell to rest against the corner of her mouth.

'I've missed you—so much,' she said wistfully.

There was a wealth of warmth in his smile as he leant his forehead down on hers, then his lips slid down to her temple before seeking the pulsing cord at her neck.

Sara felt hauntingly vulnerable, aware of each separate nerve-end as his mouth followed a tantalising exploration of the hollows at the base of her throat.

'You're my life, the very essence of my existence,' he professed softly, raising his head to gaze deeply into her radiant eyes. 'How could you not have guessed you had my heart, when every time I made love to you it was almost an act of worship?' He placed a brief hard kiss on her unsuspecting lips, then he gave a wry smile. 'It wasn't for Ana's benefit I married you, *querida*, but my own. Yes,' he added gently, dismissing her incredulity with a shake of his head, 'fate allowed me to dangle Selina's attachment to your late father's home in front of your nose like a persuasive ploy. Given time, I knew I could win your affection. What I didn't bargain for was your stubborn resistance to distinguish love from lust.' His dark eyes clouded with something like regret. 'There were some bad moments – times when I alternated between the deep aching need to love you, and the desire to shake you senseless for being so blind.'

'And now?' she teased.

'Minx!' he said gently, giving her a slight shake, then he bent to bestow a lingering kiss on her softly parted mouth before reaching for the zip fastening at the back of her dress. 'I should punish you until you weep for the pretty dance you've led me!'

Sara felt his fingers unclasp her bra, and she lifted her arms and wound them round his neck, revelling in the taut hard lines of his muscular frame as she clung to him. 'Love me, Rafael,' she whispered unashamedly. 'I *need* you.'

His response was swift and fierce as his mouth covered hers with bruising intensity, then he lifted his head to regard her, and she felt herself drown in the wealth of emotion in those dark eyes. 'Never again will you have reason to leave me, Sara,' he vowed gently. 'That I can promise you.'

A deep heartfelt sigh left her lips, and she reached for him, then she rapidly became swept up in the tide of his passion as he led her unerringly towards the heights of sensual ecstasy, and it was a long time before she lay drowsily at peace in the circle of his arms, secure in the knowledge that she had at last come home.

ROMANCE

Variety is the spice of romance

Each month, Mills & Boon publish new romances. New stories about people falling in love. A world of variety in romance – from the best writers in the romantic world. Choose from these titles in July.

FORGOTTEN LOVER Carole Mortimer
LATE HARVEST Yvonne Whittal
STARTING OVER Lynsey Stevens
BROKEN RHAPSODY Margaret Way
BLIND MAN'S BUFF Victoria Gordon
LESSON IN LOVE Claudia Jameson
MIDNIGHT LOVER Charlotte Lamb
STORM CYCLE Margaret Pargeter
PACIFIC PRETENCE Daphne Clair
WILDFIRE ENCOUNTER Helen Bianchin
THE OTHER BROTHER Jessica Steele
THE MAGNOLIA SIEGE Pamela Pope

On sale where you buy paperbacks. If you require further information or have any difficulty obtaining them, write to: Mills & Boon Reader Service, PO Box 236, Thornton Road, Croydon, Surrey CR9 3RU, England.

Mills & Boon
the rose of romance

Romance

*M*asquerade
Historical Romances

Intrigue excitement romance

THE CHIEFTAIN
by Caroline Martin

The young widow Isobel Carnegie is much sought after for her beauty as well as her fortune. But when she is kidnapped by the Highland Chieftain Hector MacLean, is he really only interested in her money?

TO CATCH AN EARL
by Rosina Pyatt

The beautiful, and immensely wealthy, Miss Dominga Romero-Browne is determined to marry the Earl of Deversham. But the Earl's heart belongs to another, so how can Dominga, once she is the Countess of Deversham, hope to win more than a title?

FREE-an exclusive Anne Mather title, MELTING FIRE

At Mills & Boon we value very highly the opinion of our readers. What <u>you</u> tell us about what you like in romantic reading is important to us.

So if you will tell us which Mills & Boon romance you have most enjoyed reading lately, we will send you a copy of MELTING FIRE by Anne Mather – absolutely FREE.

There are no snags, no hidden charges. It's absolutely FREE.

Just send us your answer to our question, and help us to bring you the best in romantic reading.

CLAIM YOUR FREE BOOK NOW

Simply fill in details below, cut out and post to: Mills & Boon Reader Service, FREEPOST, P.O. Box 236, Croydon, Surrey CR9 9EL.

— — — — — — — — — — — — — — —

The Mills & Boon story I have most enjoyed during the past 6 months is:

TITLE _____

AUTHOR_____ BLOCK LETTERS, PLEASE

NAME (Mrs/Miss) _____ EP4

ADDRESS_____

_____

_____ POST CODE _____

Offer restricted to ONE Free Book a year per household. Applies only in U.K. and Eire. CUT OUT AND POST TODAY – NO STAMP NEEDED.

Mills & Boon
the rose of romance